Rapacity & Rancor: A Pride & Prejudice Variation

Crime & Courtship, Volume 1

Abbey North

Published by Abbey North JAFF Books, 2022.

RAPACITY & RANCOR: A PRIDE & PREJUDICE VARIATION

First edition. February 10, 2022.

Copyright © 2022 Abbey North.

ISBN: 979-8215371206

Written by Abbey North.

Blurb

Meryton is atwitter with the arrival of Mr. Bingley and his friends, but Mr. Darcy leaves a bad first impression on the attendees of Assembly ball. It's almost enough to detract from the theft that occurs while everyone is inside dancing. Soon enough, other thefts occur through the village. Ever curious, Lizzy ventures to find the thief, acquiring an unexpected ally in the endeavor in Fitzwilliam Darcy. As they work together, she gains a more favorable impression of him, but he is the last man with whom she would ever want to solve another crime.

This is part one of the of the "Crime & Courtship" series, which will be five books, intended to be read in order, and follow roughly the same timeline and location as J.A.'s masterpiece. The first mystery takes place in Meryton. The next will be at Netherfield, followed by Hunsford, then London, and finally Pemberley. The story arc will continue throughout all five parts, compromising one long read broken into five parts. A mystery is central to each installment, so you could call this a cozy mystery sweet Regency romance.

While Abbey sometimes writes sensual JAFF, this series is strictly SWEET.

Chapter One

"It is most distressing," said Madame St. Croix in her French accent before dabbing her face with a handkerchief lined with lace, provided by Pierre, her husband. "I come to this country to escape the guillotine, but I am not safe here either."

"It is not as bad as that," said Lady Lucas as she patted Meryton's modiste on the arm. "You are perfectly safe."

"I have been violated."

Lizzy and Jane shared a look. Jane's was full of compassion, which didn't surprise Lizzy. Of course, she felt sorry for the seamstress as well, but having a few yards of lace, no matter how expensive, stolen from her store was hardly on par with fearing for her life as she had during the French Revolution. "Do you suppose it's anti-French sentiment?" she whispered to Jane.

Jane, using her fan to block her mouth, said, "It is quite possible. I do recall those hooligans harassing her last year."

Lizzy nodded, remembering the boys in question. Two of the three families had taken their sons to task, but the third had expressed support for their boy's actions and had told the madame to return to France.

Though they were in the midst of war with France, Lizzy couldn't blame Madame St. Croix for the actions of the men in charge who'd decided to draw arms against each other. To her way of thinking, it was grossly unfair to target the woman just because she had moved to Meryton after leaving France. She and her husband, the milliner, were both lovely people, and they didn't deserve to be targeted for harassment or theft.

Lizzy was aware of Lord and Lady Lucas continuing to try to comfort Madame St. Croix, a robust woman with a ruddy complexion, who stood in front of her slender husband. With Pierre's oversized head, he always vaguely looked like he might topple over from the weight of it, and Lizzy sometimes wondered why he'd chosen such a profession intended to draw attention to the feature by designing hats.

The St. Croixs and their drama fled her mind when there was a stir in the crowd, and Jane stiffened beside her, practically buzzing with excitement. Lizzy knew her sisters and every other single girl at the Assembly ball were atwitter with the thought of the new tenant at Netherfield, Mr. Bingley, bringing twelve women and seven men with him to the Assembly ball.

Lizzy wouldn't pretend she wasn't at least moderately interested in seeing the seven men, but she wasn't as eager for a beau as her sisters and many of the other women in the room. For her part, she would happily remain unmarried for life unless she found deep and true love, the kind she could be assured would last. Otherwise, a woman was foolish indeed to give up control of her life to a man unworthy of the trust placed in him.

She was amused when the Bingley party arrived, unsurprised to find gossip had amplified their numbers greatly. Rather than the nineteen expected, there were three men and two women. Lizzy was happy to have her fan, because she used it to shield her face as she wrinkled her nose. She didn't like to make spontaneous judgments, but the expression on the women's faces suggested they had just stepped out of their carriage into a fresh pile of horse manure. Already, they were judging Meryton's modest Assembly ball, and Lizzy felt defensive in response.

She struggled to put aside her quick conclusions, hoping it was simply culture shock for the two women, who no doubt spent most of their time in London among the *ton*. Meryton must seem quaint to them, and she tried to be understanding of that.

It took some time before the party started to move among the attendees already in place. Lizzy was unsurprised, though no less embarrassed, by her mother's usual tactics of finding her daughters and forcing them through the crowd, almost like a battering ram. She endured it, simply because she must, because that was her mother's way.

Fanny Bennet cleared her throat loudly, interrupting the conversation with Lord Lucas and the two men standing near him. The third man stood in the corner with the two women, while one of the women gazed around the room, looking no less supercilious than she had the moment she walked in.

With her pale complexion, sprinkle of freckles across her nose, and lovely red hair, she was quite a stunning sight, but Lizzy wondered if she ever smiled, and if so, could it be a genuine emotion? Was the woman trying to be fashionably aloof, or did she genuinely consider herself above everyone attending?

"Ah, Mr. Bingley and Mr. Darcy, allow me to introduce one of our fine families from the district. This is..." He trailed off, looking around. "Where is Mr. Bennet, Mrs. Bennet?" he asked in a pseudo-whisper.

Fanny looked around for a moment before waving a hand. "No doubt, he sneaked out the back to avoid interactions. It matters not, for Mr. Bingley has already met him."

Mr. Bingley spoke then, the blond man who'd seemed unable to look away from Jane until just that moment. "Yes, a delightful man, with an interesting sense of humor."

Lizzy's lips twitched. She could well imagine, since her father definitely had a humor that wasn't to everyone's taste. That she shared it was probably why she was proud of him for displaying it and intrigued Mr. Bingley had actually noticed.

Very few of the people with whom she interacted—admittedly a small circle consisting mainly of Meryton and occasional visits to the

Gardiners in London, or Charlotte in Hunsford—were likely to catch her father's dry undertones, gentle sarcasm, and occasional poking of wit at others, though not in what she deemed a malicious way.

"He is most vexing," said Fanny. "The things that man has done to my nerves."

Jane gently nudged their mother on the shoulder. "You have not been properly introduced yet, Mama." She said the words practically from the side of her mouth.

Fanny flushed for a moment, and she fell silent. Lord Lucas, used to her mother, didn't seem to notice the lapse in manners as he completed the introductions. Lizzy was viewing it all with interest, and of course, she said the right things when it was her turn to greet Mr. Bingley and Mr. Darcy.

When she locked gazes with Mr. Darcy's dark eyes, she had a moment where it was difficult to breathe. She flicked open her fan and swished her wrist to create a breeze. It was abruptly dreadfully stuffy in the Assembly ballroom.

"May I request the next two free dances, Miss Bennet?" asked Mr. Bingley of her sister.

Jane flushed in a becoming way and nodded. "I would be most pleased, Mr. Bingley."

Lizzy stood nearby as the conversation continued, painfully aware of each gauche or embarrassing thing her mother uttered. There was no changing Fanny Bennet, so Lizzy strove to accept her as she was, but it was dreadfully trying at times.

When the music for the current dance ended, Jane and Mr. Bingley took to the dance floor, and Lizzy drifted away, since Mr. Darcy was returning to his party as well. She hadn't entertained the idea he might ask her to dance until just then, and she giggled at the thought. His stiff posture suggested his governess must have taped a broom handle to his spine and forgot to remove it all these years later, so she couldn't imagine him as the dancing type anyway.

Lizzy decided to sit down, joining her sister Mary, though Mary didn't look up from the book she was reading. Of course, it was "Fordyce's Sermons," and Lizzy wondered how she could continue to read the book over and over. Lizzy had favorite books she could read a million times, but she'd never seen the appeal of Fordyce's dry sermons.

It was at times like these she missed her dear friend, Charlotte. Charlotte, daughter of Lord and Lady Lucas, had been gone three years now. She had married Lizzy's cousin, saving Lizzy from the fate by unexpectedly gaining Mr. Collins's attention when Lizzy had refused his offer.

At a mere seventeen at the time, even then Lizzy had known she didn't want to marry for anything but love. Accepting Mr. Collins had been a repulsive idea to contemplate. Despite her mother's heavy pressure, wanting one of her daughters to marry the man who would inherit Longbourn after Papa's death, Lizzy had refused the proposal when it inevitably came, though she had done her best to discourage him from ever making the offer to start with.

Fortunately, Charlotte had seemed content with the match, and she now lived in Kent, so they saw each other rarely. Lizzy always visited twice per year. Occasionally, Charlotte would come for a visit to Meryton to see her parents, so they might see each other three to four times a year, but that wouldn't be happening this year, since Charlotte was approaching her time of confinement in the next few months.

Lizzy shuddered at the thought of how the child had come to be, quickly blocking that thought. She understood enough of the basics to grasp what Charlotte must have done with Mr. Collins, and she did not want to think of that. Instead, she occupied herself with people-watching for a time, and then she grew bored with that.

Deciding a cup of ratafia would be most refreshing, she stood up, murmured a word to Mary that was not returned, and moved to the refreshment table. As she got into position with her cup, she heard whispers behind her. She cocked her head slightly, curiosity getting the better of her.

Perhaps if they'd been speaking in normal tones, it wouldn't have caught her attention at all. Since the exchange was discreet, implying someone wanted secrecy, Lizzy's natural instincts were to discover the secret itself. It wasn't one of her more flattering characteristics, but she had long ago accepted her own inquisitive nature. That her father had encouraged it, pleased when she asked questions and thought beyond the surface, only served to strengthen her determination to hold onto the trait despite Fanny's best efforts to stamp it out.

"I say, Darcy, you are standing in the corner and glowering at everyone with condemnation. My dear man, you look like a disapproving flowerpot."

Lizzy had to stifle a laugh by clenching her teeth and taking a deep breath. She recognized Mr. Bingley's voice as the one sharing that information with his friend.

"I care not a whit for how I appear, Bingley."

"I am simply saying you might try something new, like having fun, Darcy. There are lovely ladies here, and a shortage of men. It seems quite a shame for you to deny these girls the dances they are due."

"You have been monopolizing the only girl of fair appearance here. There are no handsome women remaining, and I am in no mood to sacrifice myself to dance with undesirables when other men cannot be bothered."

"Balderdash. It is not that they are not bothered. They are simply outnumbered."

Lizzy's lips twitched as she wondered if Mr. Bingley realized how unflattering that sounded.

There was a droll hint of humor in Mr. Darcy's voice when he said, "Allow me to decline to be the fortification that rescues them."

So far, Lizzy was just amused, but she froze with Mr. Bingley's next words.

"What about Miss Jane's sister, Miss Elizabeth? She is quite a handsome girl."

Mr. Darcy didn't speak for a moment. "Which one is she?"

"The one who stood next to Jane."

"I confess I barely remember anyone except for their mother. Dreadfully appalling woman."

Lizzy almost nodded in agreement, but she was too anxious to hear what his opinion of her was to do so.

"I do believe I recall a pair of fine eyes. Otherwise, it was a rather drab impression she left, and I fear she's not handsome enough to stir me to a task I do not wish to undertake. Do leave me be, Bingley, and cease further attempts to force me onto the dance floor with every farmer's daughter and tradesman's offspring that crosses your path."

Lizzy didn't wait to hear Bingley's response. Instead, she set down the punch glass without bothering to fill it. She was irritated, but by the time she'd crossed the floor after seeing Jane, she was mostly amused. She spent a few minutes sharing with her sister what had occurred, and she was hardly surprised when Jane said, "Perhaps he is tired from travel. I am certain he did not mean to offend you."

"I am certain he did not mean for me to overhear his true opinion, but I doubt that changes the fact he holds it." She looked up and saw Mr. Bingley approaching, so she made herself scarce. "Good luck with that one, as he seems to be a much better cut of cloth than his friend."

"Lizzy, you must not assume—"

Lizzy waved a hand. "Yes, I am certain he was appallingly exhausted. It probably took all the effort he could muster to insult not just me but every other woman at the ball, save you."

Jane looked exasperated, but she had no time to continue chastising her as Mr. Bingley reached her side. He extended a cup of punch, and Lizzy wished she'd taken time to serve herself ratafia after all.

She was still seething with something she decided to label amusement as she walked among the members of the ball. She knew them well, having spent all her life in the area, so she'd been to several of the Assembly balls since being introduced to society at the age of fifteen. Most found her comments about Mr. Darcy amusing, though she could see more than one resident become irritated by his denouncement of the quality of the women available.

By the time the Assembly ball had started to end, Lizzy noticed no one had approached Mr. Darcy. The haughty man likely didn't realize he was being shunned, but she could see the evidence of it. Perhaps she should've felt bad about her role in the situation, but all she had done was relay his own words. They had damned him to be ostracized and deemed irredeemably rude and entirely too proud.

Only Lord Lucas had attempted to defend him, saying, "Of course the man is proud. He comes from fine stock and has an income of ten thousand per year. I challenge you not to be so exacting in your standards were you in his Wellingtons." Before he could finish the thought, Lady Lucas had pointed out he should have exquisite manners with all the advantages ten thousand per year could offer. Lizzy had heartily nodded in agreement, though she hadn't contributed verbally to that exchange.

Kitty and Lydia were still engrossed with flirting with the officers as she looked around for Jane. Her sister was still speaking with Mr. Bingley, and they now stood near the two women who had accompanied Mr. Bingley to the Assembly ball. From gossip circulating the room, Lizzy had learned they were Miss Caroline Bingley and Mrs. Louisa Hurst. Both were Bingley's sisters, and the other man was Mr. Hurst, Louisa's husband. Lizzy's opinion of them remained unchanged, having observed them off and on throughout the evening. They were clearly here on sufferance, and they made little attempt to hide that.

They must have been quite special specimens indeed though. They were the only two women with whom Mr. Darcy had deigned to dance. To Lizzy's mind, they were all cut from the same cloth, and it was so rarefied and expensive a fabric that it was much too precious to contemplate wearing on a daily basis.

There was a sudden upset in the crowd as Mrs. Hofstetter let out a shrill cry. Lizzy was among the first to exit the Assembly ball, since she'd stood close to the exit. At first, she expected to find the woman in mortal peril from the way she'd cried out, but rather, she stood near her carriage pleating the handkerchief in her hands. "It is gone."

"What is gone?" Lord Lucas pushed his way through the crowd, his considerable bulk aiding him in the endeavor as he approached the carriage. "What has you upset, Mrs. Hofstetter?"

Tears were streaming down her face. "The necklace my dear Harry gave me, the very last gift he gave me the Christmas before he died. Remember how he died at the New Year three years ago?" There was a suitable round of nodding and murmurs of sympathy from the crowd, including Lizzy, and the widow continued, "I do cherish it so, but I noticed this evening that the clasp was weak, so I decided to leave it in the carriage to avoid the risk of losing it while I was in the ball. It was right here on the seat, but now it is gone."

"Could it be taken by your driver?" asked one of the men in the crowd.

Mrs. Hofstetter was clearly offended at the question. "Nonsense. Hill has been our driver for at least twenty years."

Lizzy's gaze darted to the man, and she recognized him as their housekeeper's nephew. She didn't know the man well, but she couldn't imagine he was dishonest if he came from the same family as fine Mrs. Hill.

"It must have been misplaced," said a woman. Lizzy couldn't identify who from the crush of the crowd.

"I tell you, I left it right where it was easy to see, but it is gone. Someone has stolen it."

There was a murmur of unease as the crowd echoed what Lizzy was feeling. She instantly recalled Madame St. Croix's words from earlier, and she couldn't help wondering if there was something more to the thefts than anyone realized. Was there a common link? Or was Mrs. Hofstetter's necklace missing for another reason, and had Madame St. Croix simply been targeted for being French?

It seemed more than coincidental, and Lizzy's mind continued to work over the problem long after the ball had ended, and she and Jane were back in the room at Longbourn, having talked through the evening before Jane fell asleep. Lizzy wished for the same, and she closed her eyes, determined to count every sheep in the fields of Longbourn if necessary to attain restful slumber.

Chapter Two

Lizzy's heart fluttered as Mr. Denny approached with a soldier whom she had yet to meet. She knew he had been in Meryton as long as the other soldiers, but she'd had no occasion to cross his path yet, since she wasn't one for flirting with the soldiers like her sisters were. Still, she had noticed the handsome young man with his artfully arranged dark curls and soulful eyes. When he paused before them, his smile was warm enough to curl her toes. She held out her hand as Mr. Denny made the introductions.

"Miss Elizabeth Bennet and Miss Jane Bennet, this is George Wickham. I do not believe you have interacted with him yet?"

"No, we have not," said Lizzy, gasping softly when the other man took her hand and pressed his lips against the back of her glove. It was an unexpected reaction to such a banal touch.

"Indeed we have not, for I would never forget two such lovely ladies. Of course, I have seen you around before, but we have had no opportunity to meet. When I saw you approaching this day, I practically insisted that my dear friend, Mr. Denny, introduce me to you." His gaze moved hastily to Jane before quickly returning to Lizzy. "To both of you."

"We were on our way to our aunt's house for tea before stopping by the store. Would you care to join us?" asked Lizzy.

Jane seemed surprised by the forward invitation, but if Mr. Denny or Mr. Wickham found it too bold, they showed no signs of it.

"We shall be delighted. Mrs. Phillips does have the most exquisite lemon scones, Wickham. You shall have to try them. "

"I do look forward to it, though I have no taste for lemon." He grimaced. "It was often served where I grew up at Pemberley. Lemon was a favorite of Mr. Darcy's. The senior Mr. Darcy, not the younger one. That man is sour enough without needing to add lemons to the equation." He flushed. "Pardon my blunt speaking."

Lizzy giggled. "Are you referring to Fitzwilliam Darcy?"

Wickham frowned. "You know of him?"

"I know him as well as one can know one who refuses to make themselves open to being known." At his look of confusion, she said, "He was at the ball last evening. Did you not attend and see him there?"

Wickham frowned. "I was busy with duties. Alas, I was unable to attend. Had I been, I would have boldly asked for at least two dances on your card."

Lizzy felt like her face was on fire, and she flicked open her fan to generate a breeze. "I certainly would have been daring enough to grant the request, Mr. Wickham."

He smiled, his pleasure obvious. "Indeed, that is the Darcy to whom I refer. Would it surprise you to learn we grew up almost like brothers?"

Lizzy's eyes widened. "Indeed, it would." There were many questions on the tip of her tongue, though far too impertinent asked. She wondered how a man who'd grown up like a brother to Darcy could become a soldier in the militia.

He looked sad for a long moment. "My father was Mr. Darcy's trusted advisor and steward. Mr. Darcy had quite a soft spot for me, and when my father died, he took me in. He educated me and treated me like a child of his own." Mr. Wickham's gaze darted around for a moment, and he lowered his voice quietly, ensuring only Lizzy heard as they slowed their pace while nearing Aunt Phillips's house. "I do believe Mr. Darcy actually loved me all the better than he did his own son. That was quite tragic really, and it left Mr. Darcy jealous and angry with me. As soon as he had the chance, he struck out with revenge in mind."

Lizzy gasped, though she shouldn't be shocked that Mr. Darcy had done such a thing after seeing his display the night before. "What did he do?"

They were hanging back now, and they would soon have to join the others to enter her aunt's residence, or there would be questions as to why they were dawdling. "His father had promised me a living as the vicar at Kympton, but when he died, Darcy denied me my due and sent me away."

Lizzy was outraged on his behalf. "How dare he?"

Mr. Wickham sighed. "Perhaps he did me a kindness. Before his betrayal, I had operated under the assumption that all men kept their word, and life would always be fair. I believe I would have been a good vicar, but perhaps I wouldn't have given practical, worldly advice, for my eyes had not been opened. I shall never know, of course, for I had to make my own way in the world."

"It looks like you have done so smartly, Mr. Wickham." She nodded as she sent him a confident smile, looking up as Aunt Phillips appeared in the doorway. "We must go in."

"Yes, we must."

Lizzy led the way, still outraged on Mr. Wickham's behalf. Throughout the tea, he told her more about Darcy, painting a picture she found easy to believe. He'd been a harsh, demanding child, always considering Mr. Wickham far beneath him, and try as his father had, along with a series of governesses, since none had been able to stomach the Darcy heir for long, none of them could instill humility or compassion.

By the time they had finished tea, she was quite certain her initial opinion of Mr. Darcy had been far too generous. He wasn't simply prideful. He was arrogant, cruel, and enjoyed watching those beneath him suffer. She was appalled to have a man like that in Meryton, and further appalled that he was apparently a close confidant of the man Jane was clearly growing a *tendre* for.

As they finished tea, Jane and Lizzy stood up. "We must go by the shop. We promised Mrs. Hill we would bring her a few things, though I suspect she took pity on us and set us the task so we would have an excuse to leave Longbourn. Mama's nerves are frayed, so she has requested a quiet day," Jane said that with a delightful smile, and as always, it made everyone else in the room smile too. It was a rare person indeed who was impervious to Jane's cheerful demeanor when she displayed it—which was often.

"We must depart as well," said Mr. Denny, looking regretful. "We have duties to which we must attend as our leisure time is ending."

Mr. Wickham nodded, and he paused, running his hand lightly down Lizzy's arm in an impertinent fashion she quite enjoyed. "I would very much like to see you again, Miss Bennet."

She beamed at him. "You should come for tea tomorrow if you are free then. I am certain Mr. Denny can help you find Longbourn, as he has been a guest in the past."

He smiled. "I very much look forward to that, and I shall do my best to ensure I am free. Until we meet again, Miss Bennet." He took her hand and brought it to his mouth, kissing the back of the glove again before releasing her.

He was quite dashing, and she thought of him as she followed Jane to the general store. Perhaps she could have spent all day indulging in girlish fantasies of Mr. Wickham, setting aside the practical matter that a soldier could hardly afford to keep a wife without a sizable dowry to make it a possibility, so any long-term romance between them was doomed, but she was distracted when they entered the general store, overhearing a conversation between Jeffrey Barker, who owned the only tavern in town, and Henry and Etta Spruill, who ran the general store.

"Whoever the brute was, he must have had a handcart or been quite strong, as those barrels weigh about seven stone each." Mr. Barker was a jowly man, and his cheeks moved in an almost hypnotic fashion as he spoke.

"Pardon the intrusion, but of what do you speak?" Lizzy asked, unable to curb her curiosity.

If Mr. Barker found it impertinent, he didn't refuse to answer. "Some blimey... Some bloke stole an entire barrel of whiskey." He looked angry for a moment, and then he laughed. "I'd be much more upset if it were the expensive stuff, but this is the rotgut served to the drunks who're too pissed to notice."

He flushed suddenly, his ears turning bright red. "Pardon the language, ladies." Now looking shy, or more likely just chastened, though Lizzy had not taken him to task for the lapse, he quickly muttered an excuse and rushed from the store.

Chapter Three

Lizzy was impatient with excitement, pacing around the sitting room until she saw a flash of red coming up the drive. Then she hastily took a seat at the settee, sending a death glare to Kitty when her little sister would have sat beside her. Muttering something distinctly unladylike, though the words were incomprehensible, Kitty chose the opposite settee instead, throwing herself down with what appeared to be abject despair in a faithful display of true teenage drama.

She could hear their guests' voices in the hallway. Seconds later, Mr. Denny, Mr. Wickham, and Mr. Olson entered the room. After appropriate greetings, she was unsurprised when Mr. Wickham sat down beside her, though he left a proper space between them. She had been hoping he would take that seat, and she was gratified he had.

At that moment, Jane came in. "Pardon me for being late, Mr. Bingley—" She trailed off as she looked around. "Where is Mr. Bingley?"

Lizzy frowned. "I do not know. Did you expect him?"

"I was. I invited him for tea this afternoon." She looked briefly disappointed before rallying herself and crossing the room to take a seat in one of the free chairs. "I am certain he shall turn up."

Before Lizzy could share her assurance that she doubted Mr. Bingley would miss a chance to spend time with Jane, there was another knock at the door. Only when she heard the rumble of more voices as they spoke with Hill did she realize Mr. Bingley wasn't coming alone. He must have brought Mr. Darcy with him, and she stiffened with dismay.

Abruptly, she realized Wickham was stiff as well, and she patted him on the knee discreetly for a moment, trying to send him a silent sign of support as his nemesis entered Longbourn's sitting room. Mr. Bingley seemed at ease, but Mr. Darcy looked like he wished to be anywhere else. When his gaze fell on Wickham, he paled and appeared like he might be on the verge of bolting. She supposed a guilty conscience could do that to one, and she hoped he gave in to the impulse.

After a moment, his spine stiffened—a feat which should have been impossible with the imagined broomstick taped to it—and he crossed the room. He displayed the perfunctory level of manners as he took a seat beside Lizzy in the armchair nearby. Mr. Bingley was sitting on the other seat near Jane, and Lydia was soon handing out teacups.

At first, conversation was stilted, but then Charles, Jane, and Kitty seemed to find their groove. Mr. Denny and Mr. Olson were both talkers as well, and Lizzy was content to remain quiet, observing Mr. Darcy's discomfort with amusement she could hardly stifle.

Mr. Wickham was at his most charming, and at first, she was charmed by it. It was only when she caught him sending a challenging glance to Mr. Darcy before he reached out to blatantly touch her wrist in a far too familiar fashion that she realized perhaps Mr. Wickham wasn't as enchanted with her as he was with shocking or annoying Mr. Darcy. She frowned at the thought and quickly moved her wrist away from his fingers. "More tea, Mr. Darcy?" she asked in a cool tone.

He had been stirring his cup for a while, but she'd yet to see him lift it for a first sip. "I do not require more now. Thank you, Miss Bennet."

She nodded, turning to Mr. Wickham. "Would you like more tea, Mr. Wickham?" Her voice was noticeably cooler to him than it had been, but he didn't seem to realize.

"If poured by your lovely hand, I would happily drink a liter of it."

Mr. Darcy snorted softly, covering it with a cough, and Lizzy had the unexpected urge to look at him and share a laugh. His recognition of Mr. Wickham's charming superficiality in no way mitigated what he had done to the other man though, so she had no wish to regard him as any sort of ally.

When they had finished tea, Lydia said, "I would find a walk refreshing. Would anyone like to join me?" Mr. Denny immediately volunteered his services, and Mr. Olson quickly invited Kitty to walk along with him as well.

"I am always up for a walk," said Lizzy, recognizing she needed to play chaperone.

"I shall walk with you," said Mr. Wickham.

Lizzy nodded, accepting the invitation with not nearly as much enthusiasm as she'd had while she awaited his arrival less than an hour before. Now that she could see past his charming veneer, she wondered what was authentic about Mr. Wickham. Perhaps Mr. Darcy had good reason to dislike the man, but she could find no justification for withholding the living his father had promised. If only the man had put it in his will instead of just making his intention known, assuming his son would carry out his duty.

Realizing how Mr. Wickham had been abused, she found herself softening toward him again and accepted his arm when he offered it as they started walking. Mr. Darcy was not with the party, and she told herself she didn't care where he ended up. Perhaps he was already headed back to Netherfield, or maybe he was in the sitting room still discussing trivialities with her mother. She could hardly imagine he would voluntarily stay behind to spend more time with Fanny Bennet, and she giggled at the thought.

Mr. Wickham smiled. "May I know what has entertained you so, Miss Bennet?"

"I was simply imagining Mr. Darcy at the mercy of my mother for a time, just the two of them."

He shuddered. "Your poor mother."

"Perhaps poor Mr. Darcy."

As they shared a laugh, Mr. Wickham paused for a moment. He reached into his jacket, looking around furtively. "Pardon this, but I find myself in need of something to brace me after the experience of sharing the same air in the room with Mr. Darcy for almost an hour." He unscrewed the lid of the silver flask he'd removed from his coat and took a long drink. He eyed it hesitantly before looking at her. "I don't suppose you...?"

Lizzy frowned. "No, thank you." She struggled not to sound scandalized at the offer. She tried to view it as flattering instead, that Mr. Wickham might assume she was a girl who was prone to dance along the edges of the rules of society. That wasn't entirely untrue, but she had no interest in tasting the foul-smelling alcohol in his flask. She wrinkled her nose as he screwed on the lid. "Does it always smell that bad?"

He laughed. "With what I can afford on a soldier's salary, it does."

She patted his arm. "In that case, I am doubly sorry for what Mr. Darcy has done to you, if that is all you can drink." Sharing a laugh, they continued together, and though she didn't find him as charming as she had before, she still found Mr. Wickham quite likable, especially when contrasted with the disdainful Fitzwilliam Darcy.

Chapter Four

Lizzy occupied herself the next day with her usual morning walk and then spent part of the day reading in the library with her father. Jane had been invited for tea at Netherfield, so she wasn't there to speak with her. Lizzy missed her confidant, and though she loved her younger sisters, she didn't share the same bond with any of them.

Mary was far too serious and pedantic to invite close confidences, and Lydia was too capricious and careless, often blurting out any thought that crossed her mind. She was a beguiling delight, but she wasn't a good person with whom to share secrets. Kitty was far too young and lacking maturity yet, though Lizzy thought she saw moments of quiet contemplation in her younger sister. She had hopes Kitty might yet grow up to be a fairly sensible young woman if she didn't choose to emulate Lydia too much.

It wasn't that she had a secret to share, but she did want to discuss Mr. Wickham, and what feelings he inspired in her. She wished to share with Jane how she had grown briefly disenchanted with him, and how she couldn't seem to recapture the same spark of excitement to be in his presence after seeing how he had to adopted a more flirtatious manner to irritate Darcy rather than to show his appreciation for her.

There was a knock at the door, and Lizzy rose from the chair, opening the door to the library as Mrs. Hill opened the front door. She looked over her shoulder and saw a young man wearing Netherfield livery standing there. He nodded to Mrs. Hill and held out something in an envelope before turning and leaving.

Mrs. Hill closed the door and handed it to Elizabeth. "This has come from Netherfield, addressed to your mother."

"Thank you." Lizzy didn't let a little thing like that bother her. She broke the seal and opened the letter. She read briefly before telling the housekeeper, "Jane is staying overnight at Netherfield."

Fanny had sent Jane out on one of the plow horses, though the weather had clearly been about to turn, with laden clouds in the sky that suggested rain could start at any moment, and it had done so within minutes of Jane's departure. It had been by Fanny's design, of course, hoping this outcome would occur, and they would be forced to ask Jane to stay the night due to inclement weather.

Lizzy had hoped they would simply send her home in a carriage instead, both to stymie her mother's efforts just for the sheer joy of doing so, but also because she wanted to speak to Jane. She didn't want to be selfish though, and if this gave Jane a chance to spend more time with Mr. Bingley, who was surely back from hunting by now, how could she resent that?

Lizzy shared the news over dinner, enduring her mother's crowing. It was a similar situation the next morning when they sat down for breakfast, with Mrs. Bennet still going on about how her plan would likely work. No doubt, Mr. Bingley would call on Thomas in a matter of days to request his permission to marry Jane.

Lizzy barely held back the urge to roll her eyes. "They have known each other but a few days, Mama. How could they possibly be in love yet?"

"Love comes later. As long as he is infatuated with her, that is all she needs to secure marriage. Your sister is far too well-bred to acknowledge or give in to his manly needs beforehand."

Lizzy didn't know exactly what she meant, but she got the gist of it, and she didn't want to hear her mother say another word about *that*. Fortunately, her father interrupted then.

"You must be well pleased with yourself, Fanny. Your machinations have worked, and your daughter is now at Netherfield." Her father's lips twitched. "No doubt, she shall remain there as the mistress. I daresay, with the way you have planned it, she is likely to not even need to return home. We shall simply cart her trunks along the day we attend her wedding there."

"Mr. Bennet, why must you insist on teasing me so? My nerves—"

Thomas grinned. "Yes, my dear, I am well aware of your nerves. They have been my companion these many long years."

Lizzy's lips twitched as Kitty coughed to stifle a giggle. Both girls received a glare from Fanny, but she didn't rebuke the youngest Bennet daughter or Lizzy, because there was a knock at the door. Mrs. Hill bustled in a few moments later, taking the missive in her hand to Mrs. Bennet.

Lizzy wished she had gotten to it first as Fanny opened it and crowed with delight. "Oh, how marvelous."

"Is that the wedding invitation already?" asked Thomas, lips twitching again.

"Do not be silly, Thomas. Jane is ill."

Lizzy frowned. "How is that marvelous, and how can you sound so happy?"

"I am certain it is nothing more than a trifling cold from being exposed to the rain. She shall recover nicely, but in the interim, this will give her time to become further acquainted with Mr. Bingley. Indeed, this is remarkable. It happened just as I had hoped."

"Yes, your plans will no doubt result in a visit to the vicar for our dear daughter—whether it be for her wedding ceremony or her interment remains to be seen, my dear."

Lizzy was amused by her father's comment, though she wanted to be sure Jane was quite on the road to recovery before she allowed herself to laugh at his words. It seemed unlikely, but it was possible for Jane to succumb to her illness if it were severe enough. Young, healthy people died every day, so she refused to treat it as a laughing matter. "I am going to Meryton to fetch the apothecary. I shall take Mr. Jones with me to Netherfield. Have you any objection, Papa?"

"I do not. Take the carriage, my girl, and you can get Mr. Jones there that much faster."

"Thank you, Papa." Lizzy abandoned the remains of her breakfast and pushed back from the table. "I shall return with news of Jane."

"Do praise her for being a clever girl." Those words came from Fanny.

Lizzy let herself roll her eyes this time, since she wasn't facing her mother. "Yes, I shall be sure to compliment her on her ability to acquire a cold. Let us hope she can acquire a husband just as easily."

"Quite a sensible viewpoint," said Fanny, clearly missing Lizzy's sarcasm. That was hardly surprising.

It didn't take long to have the driver ready the carriage, and they reached Meryton in no time. The carriage drew up outside Mr. Jones's apothecary shop, and the driver opened the door for her, offering her a hand to step down. She was careful to steer clear of the mud underneath the step as she walked around the carriage and into the building.

She was surprised to find Mr. Jones in an agitated state. Constable Walters was with him, and she grimaced. The man was a bumbling fool, and his title was mostly honorary, gained by an advantageous, if short, marriage before his wife died. She had been a cousin of Lord Lucas's and died before she marked her first anniversary with Walters. Meryton rarely required his services, but when they did, he was inept. It was no secret among anyone who lived there.

"What has happened?" she asked Mr. Jones.

"Some of my supplies have been stolen. A ruffian took herbs, poultices, and my very best mortar and pestle, made from pure marble." Mr. Jones looked like he might cry in despair. "It was a gift from my parents, one they could ill-afford, but they were so proud of me when I set up my own shop." He sniffled. "Who would do such a thing?"

Lizzy frowned. "Yours is not the first theft of which I have heard these past few days, Mr. Jones. Have other thefts been reported to you, Constable Walters?"

Walters seemed startled to be the center of attention for a moment, and he cleared his throat. He was a balding man with pink cheeks, and though he was old enough to be her father, he looked at her in a repulsively lecherous fashion that made Lizzy glad she was wearing a Spencer coat over her modest day gown.

"Mrs. Shaw reported someone stealing a pie from her windowsill last week. Mr. Eddins had a chicken taken a couple of days ago. In that case, it was most probably a fox, though he insisted there were no holes in his fence. He kept fixating on the fact his latch was out of place. I told him he must have done that himself."

Lizzy conceded that was a possibility, but she was more inclined to trust the judgment of Mr. Eddins than Constable Walters. "What of the pie?"

He shrugged. "Probably some boys on a lark."

"What about Mrs. Hofstetter's missing necklace?"

The constable frowned. "She tried to file a report, but I assured her she simply misplaced it. She is a woman, and your fair sex cannot be relied upon to keep track of all the finer details."

Lizzy gritted her teeth, doing her best not to snap at him. "You refused to take a report of the crime?"

He shrugged a shoulder. "Though it is most likely a result of her faulty memory, what am I to do about the theft of a necklace anyway? If she wants it returned, she must place an ad offering a reward."

Lizzy understood that was the way of things, and the village constable, even if competent, could rarely recover stolen property, but Walters didn't even seem to go through the motions of being competent. "What about Mr. Barker's stolen whiskey, or the French lace missing from Madame St. Croix's shop?"

The constable shrugged. "I hadn't heard of anybody stealing from the Frenchy. As for Mr. Barker, he does serve a disreputable lot from time to time. Likely, some of his customers swindled him out of it. It happens and is a risk of the profession, I wager."

Lizzy rubbed the bridge of her nose to stave off a headache of frustration. "Do you not see a pattern though, Constable Walters? Surely, it is abnormal to have so many thefts in such a short amount of time? Does anyone know when the first theft was reported?"

Mr. Jones cleared his throat. "I believe it was several weeks ago, when someone stole a straight razor from the barber."

Lizzy hadn't heard about that, but she narrowed her eyes as she counted back the weeks. "Might that have coincided with about the time the militia arrived?"

Constable Walters shrugged. "Perhaps. What of it?"

"Perhaps our thief is a member of the militia."

Walters scowled. "What fantasy. The men in the militia are here for our protection. They certainly are not going around stealing from us, young lady. To suggest otherwise is outrageous."

"But the timing—"

"Not another word of this disrespectful drivel." The constable turned to Mr. Jones. "I have taken note of your theft, and should any evidence turn up, I will inform you. Otherwise, I suggest you place an advert, as Mrs. Hofstetter should do." He added those words in a scathing tone as he looked at Elizabeth before walking past her.

Mr. Jones seemed unsettled, but he blinked after a moment. "May I help you with something, Miss Bennet?"

Lizzy quickly explained her sister's illness and had him and a bag of his supplies in the carriage a short time later. She was anxious to check on Jane, but her mind kept returning to the thefts, looking for a pattern and half-convinced she'd already found it.

Chapter Five

Lizzy paced around the sitting room where she had been relegated upon arrival with Mr. Jones, sharing the space with Mr. Darcy, Mr. Hurst, and Mrs. Hurst. She'd heard from Mrs. Hurst that Miss Bingley was currently abed with a headache. Lizzy couldn't help wondering if it was the kind of headache that occurred when she'd realized Lizzy had arrived.

"If you do not cease your pacing, your prints will wear a new pattern into the rug, Miss Bennet," said Mr. Darcy.

She looked up, startled to hear the tone of amusement in his voice. She nodded absently, stopping her pacing as she came over to sit on the settee. It was closer to him than she'd like to be, but she squeezed her hands together and tried to endure. She sat quietly for a few minutes, not realizing she was fidgeting by pleating her skirt until Mr. Darcy said, "I fear your dress is now receiving similar treatment to our poor rug. Is any fiber safe from you, madam?"

Her mouth dropped open, and she was preparing an angry retort when she realized he was teasing her gently. She was startled by it, wondering if perhaps he was trying to distract her from her fear for Jane by the unaccustomed behavior he displayed. She'd certainly never seen anything carefree about him before, though to be fair, they had rarely interacted. Even yesterday, they had exchanged no more than a dozen words when he'd joined them at Longbourn for tea.

"I daresay any fabric you prefer shall be quite safe from me, Mr. Darcy, for I doubt we have any taste in common."

He arched a brow. "Indeed. I confess a preference for woolen socks. They are most toasty, particularly on a winter's evening, and they hold up well when one is slogging through the pond to retrieve a duck."

Lizzy frowned. "I must confess, I can hardly imagine you in that position. Would you not have a dog or servants for such things?"

He smiled. "Indeed, I have three very fine dogs, and I do have a very fine servant indeed, but upon occasion, one must fend for oneself."

"This is a skill you have managed to acquire, Mr. Darcy? You have the ability to fend for yourself?" She made no effort to hide her disbelief, in fact intensifying it in hopes he would consider it banter. She was attempting to interact with him on the same level, but on a deeper level, she really could not believe he'd ever ventured into a pond to retrieve his own duck.

"I have survived six-and-twenty years by my own devices, Miss Bennet. You should look to me for wisdom and guidance." He sounded so sanctimonious it had to be an affectation for her amusement. Surely.

She couldn't help a small laugh. "You are but six years older than me, and while you are practically a wizened paragon of wisdom, I am quite adept at taking care of myself as well."

"I do not doubt that." He was unexpectedly serious for a moment, and she wondered where his thoughts had wondered.

It chilled her that he might be thinking about her mother and father, deeming them unfit parents that had forced her to practically raise herself, as though she were a wild animal. Deciding she was overthinking it, she didn't call him on it. "You have been writing that letter for a long time, Mr. Darcy."

His lips twitched. "I am flattered you have noted the time I have spent on this letter to my dear sister, Miss Bennet. She will be joining us shortly, and I want to ensure she has everything she needs."

She smiled in a simpering fashion. "It is difficult not to notice when I have nothing else to occupy my thoughts, and you have engaged exclusively in the letter writing since my arrival."

"Not exclusively. I have managed to tear myself away long enough to look out for the excellent rug."

Lizzy was surprised by how his smile changed his face. It was most definitely the first real one he'd given her, and though it barely changed the tilt of his lips, moving them slightly upward, the motion caused a crinkling at the sides of his mouth and warmed his eyes. He was almost breathtaking, and she couldn't help wondering what he would look like in full joy.

She quickly squashed the speculation as she reminded herself he had no right to feel joy after what he had done to Mr. Wickham. After being such an insufferable boor at the Assembly ball, he merited prolonged discomfort, but for the actions against Mr. Wickham, he deserved to live his days in wretched misery.

Recalling why she so strongly objected to him, she sat back and made no attempt to further engage with him. When she started tapping her foot lightly, he didn't point out the tic to her this time, though he did say, "Your sister will be well."

She nodded, disconcerted by the soothing tone of voice he'd used. He seemed to want to take away some of her anxiety, and such concern was an unexpected thing from Mr. Darcy.

"Indeed, it is for you I fear far more than your sister," he said quietly and unexpectedly.

She blinked as she looked at him again. "I beg your pardon?"

His face was pinched now as he frowned in disapproval. "The company you keep is not good for a young woman, Miss Bennet. You would do well to preserve your reputation and heart by steering clear of a rake like George Wickham."

Lizzy gasped her outrage. "You dare criticize Mr. Wickham after what you have done?" She ignored his sharp frown. "The very hypocrisy." With a shake of her head, she got to her feet and started pacing again, this time moving to the farthest point in the library from him, so she wouldn't even accidentally interact with him.

A short time later, there was a knock at the door, and Mr. Jones entered. He held his hat in one hand and his black bag in the other. "I left medicine for Miss Jane, but I recommend she not be moved until the rattle in her lungs has dissipated."

Lizzy surged forward. "Will she be all right?"

"I see no reason to think otherwise. Miss Jane is in good health, and I have seen her but twice in her life, both times for trifling colds like this one. I expect she shall rebound within a day or two and be well enough to return home. In the interim, she must rest as much as possible, and be sure to give her the medications I have left behind. I also left instructions."

"I shall see to it," said Lizzy.

"Of course, you must stay too," said Bingley then.

Lizzy smiled at him. "Thank you, Mr. Bingley. I do appreciate your extended hospitality for myself and my sister. You could hardly have expected tea would become a three-day stay." She tried to laugh it off, but she felt self-conscious as she recalled her mother's maneuverings, which had led to this.

Mr. Bingley seemed fine with that. "Do pass along my well wishes to your sister, and I hope you shall join us for dinner. I will continue to send a servant to check on her on an hourly basis."

"Most generous of you." Lizzy didn't commit to dinner, hoping she could avoid the idea entirely. She didn't want to spend much time in the presence of the unpleasant people composing Bingley's party. Mr. Bingley himself was the exception, being a charming and open fellow, with none of the hauteur or disdain of Mr. Darcy and the others.

JANE WAS COHERENT ENOUGH to insist Lizzy go down for dinner. "It would be rude not to when they are kind enough to host us. I only wish I could join you." She paused as a deep cough racked her body.

Lizzy frowned. "I feel I should stay here with you."

Jane smiled gently. "I will be doing naught but sleeping, dear sister. If you must, you can send in a maid to sit with me while you eat, but I insist you take care of yourself."

"I could have a tray sent up."

Jane frowned. "That would simply create more work for the staff. No, you must interact and be a gracious guest. Mother would be a stickler for decorum, you know." Jane's eyes sparkled, not just from fever, as she said the words before she coughed again. It had started as a laugh before becoming the thick, raspy sound.

Lizzy tried once more. "You do not sound well. I would feel better if I stayed with you."

"I would feel better if you represented us with manners and showed we are all not from the same mold, dear sister." There was a hint of sharpness in Jane's tone that was rarely there. "Please represent the Bennet family as we should be."

Lizzy realized Jane was counting on her to make a good impression with the rest of the guests, hoping to counter whatever sense Fanny Bennet had left upon them. She thought it was already a lost cause, but she sighed in defeat, realizing this was something Jane needed from her—more than she needed her to bathe her brow or watch her sleep to ensure she didn't stop breathing. That was unlikely anyway, and this was a more tangible thing she could do for Jane. "Very well."

With a resigned sigh, she found herself leaving Jane's room a short time later and venturing through the house, guided by instructions from Mr. Fellows, the butler, to find the dining room. When she entered, Mr. Bingley and Mr. Darcy immediately stood up. After a brief hesitation, Mr. Hurst did the same, and she smiled at them while she took her seat before they returned to theirs.

"I am almost surprised to see you. I thought you would be nursing your sister. Her health is why you are here, is it not?" asked Caroline in an arch tone.

Lizzy gritted her teeth and managed what she hoped was a bland smile. "Jane insisted. She wanted to be certain I would eat so I can take care of her. She is a thoughtful girl."

"Indeed, she is. She is most kind and compassionate. I do not recall when I have met someone of her sterling character before," said Bingley.

Lizzy's lips twitched as he waxed poetically about Jane for the next minute before he finally regained control of himself. She was pleased to see her sister's *tendre* was certainly reciprocated.

"How is Miss Jane?" asked Mrs. Hurst, who seemed to simply because it was expected and not because she cared about the answer.

"She is running a fever, and she has a nasty cough. I hope Mr. Jones is correct in his assessment she shall be back to normal, or at least well enough to move home, in the next couple of days." Lizzy couldn't wait to be home and away from the oppressive party at Netherfield. If she didn't feel like Jane needed someone at her side, both as an ally and a caregiver, she would have kept herself at Longbourn to start with.

"What news is there from London?" asked Mr. Hurst abruptly, clearly done with the topic of Jane's health.

"I do not know. I did not bother to have the paper delivered here," said Bingley. He grinned, clearly unrepentant despite Mr. Hurst's obvious disapproval. "I wanted to get away from London and immerse myself in the local scene. It matters not which duke's daughter is having her coming out, or which matron insulted another at Almack's. Here, none of that is a concern."

"Whatever could be going on in this rusticated area that is more exciting than London?" asked Miss Bingley with a curl of her nose.

Before she could think better of it, Lizzy said, "We have had several thefts of late."

"That is dreadful," said Mrs. Hurst. She looked around, as though she expected them to be pillaged any moment. "Are we safe here?"

"It does not sound as if we are, dear sister," said Miss Bingley. For her impassioned outburst, she looked remarkably unaffected. "I suggest we pack up and return to London right away. Of course, you and Miss Bennet must stay here until she has recovered, Miss Eliza."

Lizzy grimaced, wondering why Miss Bingley had picked that name for her. Surely, she must have heard from someone that Elizabeth disliked it to have latched onto it. Only Charlotte called her Eliza, and that went back to the days when they would run through the lands of Longbourn or Lucas Lodge, pretending they were pirates.

Sometimes, they were princesses, though Miss Eliza and Miss Lottie were always the heroes in their pieces, not requiring a prince to rescue them. That bit of nostalgia allowed her to endure the nickname from Charlotte, and she thought about telling Miss Bingley she disliked it, but she was certain the woman would continue to use it, and at every given opportunity, if she revealed her distaste.

"I am certain you are quite safe. The thefts began a few weeks ago, and so far, they have been mostly trivial things."

"Has something changed about the area?" asked Mr. Darcy unexpectedly. "Have new people arrived, for example?"

Miss Bingley laughed uncomfortably. "Surely you are not suggesting we are the thieves, Mr. Darcy?" She laughed with a high-pitched, shrill giggle she probably thought was quite fetching.

Lizzy shuddered at the sound, but she kept her attention focused on Mr. Darcy. "Indeed, the militia arrived about that time." She braced herself, recalling Constable Walters's overreaction to the suggestion. He had acted like she'd committed treason at just the very idea of suggesting one of the militia among them might not be strictly honorable.

His lips tightened. "Interesting timing. What a coincidence. We used to have such coincidences happen at Pemberley from time to time, but then they stopped almost a decade ago."

There was surely some significance to his words, and Lizzy intuited he was perhaps implying Mr. Wickham had stolen from Pemberley. That was a foul thing to suggest, but she could hardly challenge him on it now and maintain good manners. Since she was here to represent the Bennet family on Jane's behalf, she couldn't get into an argument with her host's guest. She just ignored him, not bothering to reply to that or look at him again throughout the rest of dinner.

Chapter Six

Fitzwilliam paced around his bedchamber at Netherfield, wishing he could suppress the image of Miss Elizabeth Bennet from entering his thoughts. She was far too plain for his tastes. She wasn't ugly by any means, and there was a certain charm and grace about her when she bothered to display it. Yet when contrasted with Miss Jane or women of his acquaintance in London, she was certainly understated in appearance, and he would much prefer an Incomparable to someone so ordinary.

He couldn't deny she had a quick mind, and it was almost as sharp as her tongue. Whatever he had done to run afoul of her, she was unlikely to forgive it. Why it mattered to him, he couldn't say. She was nothing more than a country girl he should be able to quickly banish from his thoughts whenever she wasn't around—and once Miss Jane was sufficiently recovered enough to return home, she would be gone from them again. Surely, he would stop thinking about her at that point.

They'd already been at Netherfield for almost two days, and he was hopeful tomorrow Miss Jane would be able to go home. He braced himself, already having received word that evening via Miss Caroline that Mrs. Bennet intended to call on them tomorrow to see if Jane was ready to go home. He had no doubt she'd bring along her other daughters, though Thomas Bennet would likely not be with them. The man seemed to dislike social interaction, which was one commonality they shared.

Darcy preferred to engage in conversation with close acquaintances and keep his circle small. He didn't fare well with meeting new people, finding it difficult to relate to them and obtain common ground.

That must be why he was so stressed to have Miss Bennet in Charles's house. After all, he was quite familiar and close to everyone else in Bingley's party—though not as close as Miss Caroline would like, he conceded with a twitch of his lips. He did his best to dissuade her, but he feared she intended to drag him to the altar by hook or crook. That necessarily kept him on guard around her.

Yet he had found himself doing the opposite with Miss Bennet. She'd spent some time downstairs yesterday in the library, and he had engaged her in conversation again. At first, she had been cool and distant with him, but as they'd engaged in a lively discourse about the merits of Socrates's methods, she'd forgotten to hold him at arm's length, and for a few moments, they'd had true accord, though they had shared opposite opinions. That was like nothing he'd ever experienced before, and he longed to have it occur again.

That he was thinking such thoughts were dangerous, and he did his best to push them away. It would be better to prepare himself to endure the Bennet visit on the morrow than think about Miss Bennet and her fine eyes.

THE VISIT WAS AS UNPLEASANT as he had anticipated, with Mrs. Bennet being gauche and entirely too forward. She'd dared argue with him about the social scene of Meryton, contrasting it favorably with London by saying there were four-and-twenty families they dined with on a regular basis. It'd taken all he had not to laugh in her face at that point, but he did not want to be unkind.

She was beneath him in every way, including education and social standing, and he was not one to prey on the weakness of others. Unlike some that he knew, he did not find bullying gratifying or empowering.

Instead, he had somehow managed to maintain a gentlemanly façade and had even once earned a look of sympathy from Lizzy herself. That had seemed like a small victory, and he savored it now as the Bennets prepared to depart.

Miss Jane was walking between Lizzy and her mother, leaning heavily on both of them, but she looked better. Other than having to pause for a rest twice, she made steady progress to the waiting carriage a few minutes later. Darcy struggled to appear unaffected when he held out a hand to offer Elizabeth assistance into the carriage, and she took it.

Touching her was like a jolt of electricity shooting through his body, and he had to consciously focus on not tightening his hold on her hand. It took considerable effort to make himself let go when she was seated. He flexed his hand at his side, savoring the feel of the warmth through her glove. He was unexpectedly glad he'd not worn gloves himself that day, for it would have been another barrier.

He was being far too ridiculous. Feeling the need to clear his thoughts, he waited until the carriage departed before rushing to the stables. He retrieved Goliath, and the black stallion seemed eager to see him. No doubt, the horse would appreciate a good run, and after the groom prepared him, Darcy mounted, uncaring he wasn't wearing riding clothes, and let Goliath gallop away from the stables.

The horse ran quickly, and Darcy let him have his head for the most part, enjoying the freedom of a good ride for both of them. It left him feeling calmer and in a better frame of mind. She had almost fled his thoughts, or so he told himself, so for a moment, he swore he was hallucinating when he saw Lizzy as Goliath turned the corner.

She was walking ahead of them on the road, but she hadn't seen them yet. Moved by a compulsion he couldn't explain, Darcy dismounted the horse and left Goliath to graze in the field. Goliath would come when called, or he would find his way back to Netherfield on his own. He was a well-trained horse.

He thought about approaching her, but then he realized she might be sneaking into Meryton to meet with Wickham. There was an air of furtiveness about her that suggested she didn't want anyone to see her, and that was what raised his suspicions. He could not allow her to meet with Wickham. Even if she were the basest woman he'd ever met, he could not permit her to risk her reputation in such a fashion—and she was nowhere near base.

He thought about interceding, warning her away from the idea, but he knew she was unlikely to listen to him. Even if he thwarted this meeting, she would simply set up another. No, it was better to follow her, catch her in the act, and hopefully shame at least her into better behavior, because he knew there was no shame remaining in George Wickham.

He followed her at a distance, hanging back as far as he could until they reached Meryton. At that point, he felt confident moving a little closer. He was surprised when her first destination was the barbershop. What possible reason could Miss Bennet have for visiting the men's barber? He shook his head as Lizzy moved closer, thankful she had left the door open so he could overhear the conversation.

"I wanted to ask you about the theft that occurred, Mr. Cravvy."

His eyes widened at the question. It was simply unexpected, though she had no other plausible reason for visiting the barber that he could see either.

"It was a fine silver straight razor, handcrafted in Switzerland." Clearly, the barber knew exactly to what she referred, and he had no hesitation discussing it. "I bought it after saving a long time to celebrate having my shop for ten years." He sounded choked up for a moment.

"I am terribly sorry, Mr. Cravvy. Do you recall if the militia was already here when it was stolen?"

As Darcy listened, there was a pause. "I do believe they had just arrived perhaps a few days before, Miss Bennet. Why?"

"No reason," said Lizzy in a breezy fashion. "Thank you very much for your time, Mr. Cravvy. I do hope Constable Walters will find the razor."

The unseen Mr. Cravvy let out a snort. "I do not believe Constable Walters could find his as...hat with his hand."

Darcy's lips spasmed, recognizing just exactly what the barber had been about to say before he remembered himself. Realizing Lizzy was leaving, he darted around the corner. He was reluctant to be caught following her, but he still had to rule out the possibility she was meeting with Wickham.

He followed her as she went around the village, stopping to speak with a farmer, and another woman at a cottage with a thatched roof. When she stopped moving around, pausing in a nearby field to lean against a tree after speaking with the last woman, she appeared deep in thought. That was a striking look for her, and he was unable to deny the compulsion to move closer. He cleared his throat as he approached, standing respectfully before her. "Good afternoon, Miss Bennet."

Her eyes widened as she saw him standing before her, and he couldn't tell exactly what she was feeling, but he suspected dismay was the main component. "Mr. Darcy, I did not expect to see you again so soon." She sounded unhappy.

He shrugged a shoulder. "To be honest, I followed you."

Her eyes widened, and her posture straightened as she pressed her back against the tree. "I beg your pardon?"

He waved a hand. "I saw you walking to Meryton and followed. I was simply concerned you might be meeting with an undesirable party, but instead, you are questioning people. I would like to know why."

"I would point out that is none of your affair, Mr. Darcy." She glared at him.

Exasperation had him clamping his lips. "Perhaps your father would like to pose the question to you instead?"

She crossed her arms over her chest as she glared at him. "I am doing nothing that is worth blackmailing me, Mr. Darcy."

He laughed. "I am hardly blackmailing you. I am simply requesting you tell me what you are doing." He also wanted to reassure himself she wasn't meeting with Wickham.

After a moment, she sighed. "Very well. If you must know, I wanted to learn more about the robberies that happened here. I was hoping to figure out who is purloining objects from residents and businesses in Meryton. I have a theory, and I was testing it."

"Is your theory that someone in the militia is doing the thieving?"

She hardly seemed startled that he had reached the same conclusion. "I confess, my thoughts leaned that way—well before you suggested such a thing at dinner that day, Mr. Darcy." There was an air of challenge about her as she said that, and she clearly didn't want him to think she was stealing his idea or relying on a theory he had offered.

His lips twitched. "I would never have the audacity to think you might have benefited from my assistance earlier. No doubt, a woman with your lively mind had already reached that conclusion. Have you interrogated anyone in the militia yet?"

She looked uncomfortable then. "I was trying to figure out how to do so, Mr. Darcy."

"While you figure it out, perhaps we could walk to the barracks together? It you would be inappropriate for you to approach to conduct your investigation alone."

Her eyes widened, and her lips parted in the most becoming fashion that required him to tear his gaze away quickly before he started thinking about what those lips might taste like. "You are not trying to stop me?"

He frowned. "Why should I? It is not my place, and I confess I too am curious. I do wonder why a finely bred young woman such as yourself would enmesh herself into an investigation of this sordid business though?"

She seemed to think he was insulting her through subtle sarcasm. "I *am* a woman of fine breeding, and I know decorum."

He kept his tone gentle. "I was not trying to imply otherwise, Miss Bennet. I simply wondered what your motives are?"

After a moment, her shoulders relaxed, and her arms dropped to her sides as she took a step toward him. "I have been cursed with inquisitiveness. My mother has done her best to stamp out the trait of curiosity. After all, it is most unbecoming to want to know anything about the world around you and pure impertinence to question things..." She trailed off, clicking her tongue. "Most unladylike."

His lips twitched. "Yes, I am certain every gentleman would prefer a woman who plods through life without a thought in her head and makes no effort to question anything around her."

Lizzy gave him a genuine smile, and it made his chest constrict. "Now you understand, Mr. Darcy. With five daughters and no sons, my mother is most preoccupied with marrying us off, so she has endeavored to make us the best future wives possible." Apparently, she realized she was being too honest, even at the pursuit of highlighting her mother's idiosyncrasies, and she must not want to confide in him.

Her expression changed, becoming more serious. "It is simply my own nature that drives me to know what happened. That, and Constable Walters..." She trailed off with a grimace. "He is exceptionally unproductive even for a village constable. I fear the man could not find a connection between points A and B if the lines were already drawn for him."

Darcy stifled a laugh of amusement at her words. "Surely, he cannot be all that bad."

Lizzy didn't bother to reply. "If you are intent on offering assistance, I suggest we go now. There will be a change of the guard soon, and if I am not mistaken, Mr. Denny should be available for a short time. He is the soldier I know best, since he is Lydia's favorite."

Fitzwilliam held out his arm, almost surprised when she deigned to take it, and they strolled together through the streets of Meryton, moving to the barracks. They stood together quietly for a few moments as the soldiers came and went until Lizzy recognized the one she was looking for. He'd seen him at the Bennets' household before for tea, so he assumed this was Mr. Denny.

Lizzy rushed toward him, waving at him as Darcy followed right behind her. His gaze was alert for Wickham, but he saw no sign of the other man.

Lizzy spent the first few minutes talking to Mr. Denny about inconsequential things, and Darcy did his best to contribute here and there, but he wasn't one for small talk. He felt uncomfortable and unnatural. Once they had discussed the weather, the day's training events leaving Mr. Denny's calf muscles screaming with protest, and the trifle the man was looking forward to having for dessert, Lizzy asked, "Have you heard about the thefts, Mr. Denny?"

"I have heard rumblings," said Mr. Denny.

"It is a good thing the militia is here, should we find the thief in our midst. Tell me, have any of the soldiers been victims of theft?" asked Lizzy.

Mr. Denny appeared deep in thought. "Not that I...no, I take that back. Yes, Bamford had an exceptionally fine quill pen stolen from him, though I suppose it might have been misplaced. He insisted it was removed from his trunk though."

"Is that all?" asked Lizzy.

"Now that you mention it, Carson and Peters argued the other day. They were contending each had stolen the other's snuff, because their stashes were quite depleted. They share a section, so their trunks are side-by-side. I dismissed it as one of them getting into the wrong trunk, but perhaps there was more to it?"

Lizzy quickly thanked Mr. Denny for his time, and they were soon walking away. She looked dejected, and he couldn't help asking, "What troubles you, Miss Bennet?"

She blinked and looked up at him. "I was so certain it was someone in the militia, and now I do not know who it could be."

He frowned. "Why have you abandoned your original hypothesis?"

"If men in the militia have been stolen from as well, it must be someone in Meryton."

He shook his head. "Or perhaps it is one of the soldiers stealing from his own."

Her eyes widened, and she stopped in the middle of the road. "Surely, no soldier would do that to his comrades?"

Darcy shrugged a shoulder. "I am not a thief, so I cannot pretend to think like one, but it seems to me if one is willing to steal from innocent peers, especially in cases where people have little they can afford to lose, I do not think they would draw the line at stealing from people they share time with and have easy access to their items."

He had a suspect firmly in mind based on similar occurrences at Pemberley over the years, but he refused to mention the name, certain she would accuse him of unfairly judging the suspect. Surely, her mind was quick and lively, and she'd make the connection herself soon enough.

She looked uneasy, but she nodded. "Unfortunately, I believe your logic is sound. A thief is unlikely to ignore an opportunity for rapacity, is he?"

"I agree, it is most unlikely. It is a dishonorable thing to do, but I am certain there are some who are low enough for the task."

Lizzy shook her head. "Most appalling, but it does little to aid my investigation. Assuming it is someone in the militia, how will I find them?"

Darcy hesitated and then shrugged. "I do not know how to advise you. I confess, I have never investigated like this before."

Her lips twitched. "Surely you jest, Mr. Darcy. I find it highly unlikely that you cannot go to Bow Street and immediately procure a position as a Runner."

His lips twitched. "Yes, I have no doubt they would desire a man of my accomplishments."

She tipped her head, asking a little too sweetly, "What might those accomplishment be, Mr. Darcy?" The chit clearly believed he had few, if any.

He couldn't let that assumption stand. "Let us walk as I enumerate them for you."

Chapter Seven

Darcy had done his best to highlight his good points, though he thought Lizzy still seemed far too skeptical of his claims.

"You truly expect me to believe you can remember the name of every servant at Pemberley?"

He shrugged a shoulder. "Indeed, I do. They are the ones who see to my comfort, and I owe them courtesy and respect. If the people below-stairs are unhappy, those of us above-stairs will certainly feel the fallout. I recall once when I was but a young man, not quite at my majority, I insulted the cook after she had toasted my bread more on one side than the other. It was a solid three months of burnt toast before she finally forgave the insult. It required a box of chocolates and an apology to restore calm."

Lizzy laughed, and he realized she'd done that quite a few times over the intervening moments as they'd walked. "That I can believe, Mr. Darcy."

"I am happy to see you are always prepared to think the worst of me." He tried to inject his words with dry humor, but there was a part of him most melancholy about the idea, and he feared he'd revealed that when her eyes widened.

"Perhaps you have set me up to think the worst, Mr. Darcy. After all, unhandsome women like me, in need of a pity dance partner, are bound to have a low opinion of one who shares such words."

His eyes widened, and he stumbled in horror. "You heard what I said at the Assembly ball?"

She nodded. "Indeed, I did. I was not lurking or eavesdropping. I was there to get punch, and you and Mr. Bingley were on the other side of a large potted plant. I do believe Mr. Bingley complimented your ability to appear like one in fact," she said with a note of teasing.

He flushed. "I apologize for my indiscreet words. I was tired, and I do not perform as well in social situations as Mr. Bingley. It allowed me to speak with intemperate impulse."

"It hardly matters that you spoke the words aloud if you thought them." She shrugged a shoulder. "Meryton will never compare to what you are used to, but it is most unfair to judge it without granting any possibility we might have our own lures."

His heartrate accelerated for a moment, and he found it difficult to breathe. "Believe me, I understand there are certain charms in Meryton that can be found nowhere else." Namely, the young woman walking beside him. He left that unspoken, wondering if she could infer his meaning.

If so, she appeared unmoved by it, though he hoped she was simply oblivious to what he'd intended. He didn't want her to get the wrong idea. Just because he admired her brain and ability to engage in wits didn't mean anything. At most, they could be friendly acquaintances, because he certainly wasn't in the market for more.

When he took a wife, she would be of suitable breeding, and she would likely have similar wealth to him. She would not be cursed with a liability like Fanny Bennet for her mother. If his aunt had her wish, he would marry his cousin Anne, but he could not imagine doing so. She was more like a sister than anything, and any marriage to her would feel unnatural.

"May I ask you something, Mr. Darcy?" She sounded unexpectedly serious.

He paused, turning to face her as their walking ceased. "You may." He braced himself, judging he probably wouldn't like whatever she said by the way she was squaring her shoulders and seemed to be drawing in a deep breath for courage.

"Why did you deny Mr. Wickham his living when you knew that was your father's wish? It was a cruel thing to do."

His eyes widened. "I did what?" He couldn't hide his cold anger. "What did he tell you I did?" As Lizzy told him, his anger grew steadily, and his words were terse when he said, "Mr. Wickham was not suited to be a vicar."

She frowned. "He assured me your father had him educated for the role."

Darcy snorted. "It is true my father paid to send him to Oxford alongside me."

She looked troubled. "Did you resent that? It must have been difficult to have your father treating him like a son."

Darcy barely quelled the urge to roll his eyes. "My father was a warm and loving man, and he did care for George. He loved him like a son, but that didn't mean he loved me any less. Once upon a time, I was as charmed by Wickham as you, but when we were away at Oxford, I saw the real him. He was a man prone to drinking and gambling, and he was a seducer of women."

She gasped, looking outraged on Wickham's behalf. "You go too far with your allegations, Mr. Darcy. It seems unbelievable."

He snorted. "He is quite charming, but there is a viper beneath the surface. There was a young woman who cleaned rooms for us, and he left her in an indelicate way. She came to him for help, but he refused to see her. The next time someone came, it was her sister. The girl had procured a dangerous solution to the situation, and she needed help desperately. I ensured she was seen by a discreet surgeon, and then I gave the sisters money to start over away from London. I knew at that point, I could never in good conscience allow Wickham to be the spiritual leader of the people at Kympton."

She still seemed determined to disbelieve him. "That is a serious accusation."

"It most certainly is. When my father died, I was prepared to tell Wickham he would not be receiving the rectory, but he was the first to tell me he didn't want it. He freely acknowledged he wasn't a man of the right temperament for it, and he sold me a story about wanting to study the law instead.

"I gave him a bank draft for three thousand pounds, and I considered the matter closed. Apparently, he did too until he ran out of money. He tried to fleece me a couple more times, and I gave him money both times, but by the third time, I had to say no more. He had already gone through what would have been the full lifetime living and then some."

Lizzy looked startled, but she wasn't rejecting his words now. "How terrible."

"It is not the most terrible thing he did. The last time he came for money and I refused, he promised I would be sorry, and he would have his share of the Darcy inheritance one way or the other. I thought they were simply empty words until I visited my sister, who was staying for the summer in Ramsgate, and discovered her companion had been most inappropriately allowing Wickham access to her alone."

Lizzy gasped. "No."

He nodded. "I assure you, it is the truth. He had convinced her they were in love, and they were about to elope. She told me about it, expecting me to be happy for her, but when I wasn't, she was surprised. I confronted Wickham, making it clear he would never get her dowry even if he managed to compromise her. Even if he persuaded her to marry him under dishonorable circumstances like going to Gretna Green, I would refuse to acknowledge the match, at least financially. I would never cut Georgiana out of my life, but I would never do a thing to benefit his. With those words, he disappeared, leaving my poor fifteen-year-old sister heartbroken as she came to understand his love had all been false, crafted to make her fall in love with him so she would make an unwise decision."

Even reciting it was enough to make his breath catch his throat as he recalled the shattered look on Georgiana's face when she'd finally accepted he wouldn't be coming back to visit or defy Fitzwilliam's edicts. She'd accepted he didn't love her more than her dowry, so she had been despondent and cried on Darcy's lap for the rest of that afternoon. Even now, it was enough to make his blood boil again recalling the level of her agony.

Lizzy looked similarly devastated, and he couldn't hold back the impulse to put a hand on her shoulder. "I am sorry to shatter your illusions, Miss Bennet. Wickham is not someone you can trust. Before you do something foolish like fall in love with him, I can assure you now there is no way he would take you as a wife. You lack sufficient dowry to hold his interest."

After a moment, she nodded. She still looked shaky, but she wasn't rejecting the truth of his words. "I did observe he seemed more charming than usual when it appeared to irritate you, so I suppose I am not surprised he is a man different from how he presents himself. I am most aggrieved on your sister's behalf, and I thank you for enlightening me about the information before I did something foolish like come to care for the man."

Her tremulous smile underscored how quickly she was blinking, and he was certain she was seconds from crying. Deciding to do the gentlemanly thing by giving her moments to compose herself, he said "I must fetch my horse. If you wait here, I will offer you a ride the rest of the way to Longbourn."

Lizzy shook her head frantically. "I do thank you for the offer, Mr. Darcy, but I am no horsewoman. I shall walk the rest of the way."

Recognizing she needed some time alone, Darcy didn't offer to continue accompanying her. He waited until she had walked a short distance before summoning Goliath. The horse came a couple of minutes later, and he mounted and rode him, keeping enough distance between himself and Elizabeth to give her some privacy while ensuring she made it home safely. When she turned down the road for Longbourn and arrived at her drive, he rode on by, regretting any pain he'd caused her, though he knew he was saving her from a larger measure in future.

Chapter Eight

Lizzy didn't have a definite plan in mind, but she decided to return to Meryton the next day to see what else she could find from the townspeople or perhaps from the militia. She still wasn't certain how to broach that topic with any of them, for how did she introduce the idea someone among them was possibly stealing from them? It would be a gross betrayal of trust, and she could well imagine it would be a scenario where they would want to shoot the messenger.

Preoccupation with how to continue her investigation fled her mind when she saw clandestine movement ahead of her. She veered off the road to see what had caught her eye, realizing it was someone walking through the field. There wasn't much cover to observe them while hiding her presence, but as they appeared to be approaching a shack that looked like it was barely standing, she didn't feel like she had to get too close.

Still, she craned her neck over the bush from where she was hiding, attempting to make out as many details about the person as possible. She felt confident labeling them a man simply from their height and the width of their shoulders, though it was moderately possible it could be a woman.

The oversized, drab greatcoat the figure wore made it difficult to tell much about the shape, and there was a large hat pulled down over their head. Still, she thought it was a man, and he tugged on the door for a moment before a squeaking sound of warped wood scraping against warped wood shattered the silence in the meadow.

It caused a bird to cry with fright, and she looked up, almost crying out herself as the bird took flight. It had startled her, but she managed to stifle her reaction, maintaining silence while she watched the figure take something from his coat and put it inside the building. Then he closed it, and she realized he was coming her way. He would be returning shortly, and she doubted the foliage in which she hid would provide enough coverage.

Uncertainly, she looked at the tree above her, wondering if she would have time to scale it before the figure got close enough to realize she'd been spying on him. It offered her best chance, so she tucked the hem of her dress and petticoat into her bodice, grasped the branches, and scurried her way up the tree. It was much harder than she remembered, but at least she was wearing slippers with thick soles meant for walking. Recalling the ease with which she and Lottie had scrambled up trees when they were younger, she marveled it had ever been second nature.

She was breathing heavily from the exertion, but she struggled to hold her breath as the man passed underneath her. Lizzy hoped to get a look at him, eager to identify him, but the best she got was a flash of red under the greatcoat, which suggested militia to her. She tried to crane her neck to get a better look, but that undermined her already precarious position, so she clung to the branch and abandoned the idea as she pressed her back against the bark to center herself.

She waited probably far longer than necessary, but she wanted to be sure he was gone, and that no one else was around to see her departure from the tree. She scurried off the branch and slipped down, relieved to be on solid ground moments later with only a skinned palm to show for her misadventure. She pressed it against the side of her dress, wincing at the blood left behind. It was only a small scrape, and though it stung, it wasn't going to incapacitate her.

She looked around, once more ensuring the murky figure hadn't returned before crossing the field to approach the old shed he'd been using for whatever nefarious purpose.

It was a ramshackle thing that had been there at least ten winters that she could recall. The tenants who'd leased the land had been gone since their father died, and to her knowledge, her father had been unable to find a new tenant. Or perhaps, knowing Thomas Bennet, he'd simply been too buried in his books these past five years to be bothered with such a trifle.

She moved closer, having a difficult time with the latch. It wasn't that it was impervious or well-made. Rather, it was the damaged wood from exposure to moisture. When she finally got it open and tugged on the door, it made the same screeching sound she'd heard earlier that had startled the bird and nearly made her cry out.

As soon as Lizzy opened the door, she knew she'd found the cache of the Meryton thief. She hadn't seen any of the items herself, but she'd heard enough about them to recognize Madame St. Croix's beige lace that looked delicately impressive, wrapped in a length of plain muslin with a hint of the treasure beneath peeking out. It was resting atop a wooden barrel that reeked of cheap alcohol even from where she stood. There was a glittering necklace with diamonds and rubies, and a silver straight razor, among other items she hadn't even known were missing. Of course, there was no sign of the chicken or the pie, but what thief would leave those lying around? He'd likely consumed them the day of the thefts.

Lizzy considered her options as she heard a whistling sound. She jerked upright, certain it was going to be the man who'd done all the thieving returning. While she'd like to identify him, she didn't want it to be so hands-on, with just the two of them, since he was likely able to overpower her.

Her heart stopped beating for a moment, but it resumed with a faster thump when a young boy came into sight. He carried a fishing pole over his shoulder, and he was clearly intent on whiling away the hours. She waved at him, and he detoured from the road to cross the field toward her as she rushed to meet him.

"Hello, Miss Bennet, innit?" He asked with an adorably charming dimple flashing in his cheeks as he smiled.

"Indeed I am. I am afraid I do not know your name though, lad."

"I am Charlie Buckingsale. Me father's the miller."

She smiled. "A most important job. Do you anticipate following him?"

He shrugged. "I guess so. Don't know what else I'd do."

She struggled to hide her smile, not wanting him to think she was laughing at him. "I must ask you to perform a weighty task, young Charlie."

He tilted his head, looking intrigued. "What can I do for you, Miss? You must have everything."

There was something heartrending about the innocent words that recognized the class differences between them. He probably had little concept of how low the Bennets ranked overall, and she blinked back unexpected tears at the thought of him being in awe of them.

Clearing her throat, she said, "Do you think you can take a message to Netherfield?" She frowned when she said Netherfield, having intended to say Meryton. She'd planned to ask the boy to fetch Constable Walters, though it seemed a futile task. Even when confronted with all the proof of the robberies, he'd probably find some way to believe a different version than whatever Lizzy suggested.

Knowing that man, he'd probably assume it was the little boy in front of her who'd stolen everything. No, she couldn't risk his incompetence tainting the investigation. "I need you to get a message to Mr. Darcy."

"Of course, Miss Bennet."

Lizzy had no paper or ink to write, so she would have to send a verbal message. She wanted it to be something he would recognize, so he wouldn't dismiss the boy as telling tales. Finally, she said, "Could you please tell Mr. Darcy there is fabric that needs protecting? Then I would like you to bring him here. Do you think you can do that, Charlie?"

The boy looked bewildered by the message, but he nodded. "I am to tell Mr. Darcy to bring you here for fabric."

She shook her head. "No, you need to tell Mr. Darcy there is fabric that needs protecting from Miss Lizzy Bennet. Then I want you to bring him here. Do you understand?"

His face screwed up with concentration when he said, "I am to ask Mr. Darcy to come to you to protect the fabric, and I am supposed to bring him here." He beamed at her.

She ruffled his hair. "Excellent. Do run along, and hurry back. This is particularly important." As Charlie turned and ran off, she couldn't help wondering if she should've sent a different message, but she was afraid the little boy wouldn't remember something too long, and she wanted it to be specific enough that Darcy would believe it came from her. If he recalled their first conversation in the library, it would be quirky enough to hopefully get his attention and allow him to overcome any doubt to follow the boy.

Lizzy kept a wary eye around her as she waited for Darcy to come via the accompaniment of Master Buckingsale. She also watched to ensure the thief didn't return. If he did, she would have to find a hiding place or scramble up the tree if she had a chance. She was wasn't foolish enough to confront him on her own.

After what felt like forever, though was probably less than an hour, Mr. Darcy appeared in the company of little Charlie. He held the boy in front of him on Goliath's back, and Charlie was grinning with delight. It was probably the highlight of his day, if not his entire life. As soon as Darcy saw her, he drew on the reins, and Goliath's large hooves thundered onto the ground as he stopped a few feet away from her, allowing Darcy to dismount before holding up hands to lift down the boy.

Lizzy didn't want to bring Charlie into the situation any further than she had, so she knelt down to his level and said, "Thank you so much, Charlie. If you go to Longbourn this afternoon, tell Mrs. Hill Lizzy wants her to give you four of her apple tarts."

The boy laughed in delight. "Marvelous, Miss Bennet. That is one for me, Mama, Papa, and Sarah. Thank you so much." He tugged at his hat in a respectful fashion before grasping the fishing pole he'd left on the ground near Lizzy when he ran off to get Mr. Darcy.

Darcy said, "Wait a minute, young man."

Charlie halted, turning back to face Mr. Darcy. "Yes, sir?" If he was intimidated by Darcy, it didn't show.

"I believe your tie is faulty."

Lizzy looked at the boy, who was not wearing a tie. What was he talking about?

A moment later, disregarding his highly polished Wellingtons and tan breeches, Darcy knelt on the ground beside the boy and took his fishing pole. With a quick twist of his fingers, he reconfigured the way the child had tied his knot, saying, "This will make it sturdier, so it is less likely to break when you catch a fish."

"Thank you, Mr. Darcy." With a wave and a whoop of joy, the little boy ran away. Lizzy grinned after him for a moment before looking at Darcy and losing her smile. He seemed troubled. "I am sorry to send for you in such an unorthodox fashion, Mr. Darcy, but I could think of no one else to assist me."

He arched a brow while he touched his hat. "I am always happy to assist a lady."

"As I was walking to Meryton this morning, I observed a sly figure creeping about. I followed him, and he approached the shed." As she spoke, Lizzy pointed to and started walking in that direction. She drew to a halt when his hand rested on her shoulder. She turned to him. "What?"

"Have you no common sense, woman? Following a thief? You could have been gravely injured."

She scowled at him. "I hardly knew I was coming upon the situation before it happened, did I, Mr. Darcy? For your information, if I had made a big production, he likely would have noticed me more than when I ducked into the bushes. When I saw he was coming back my way, I scurried up the tree and hid there until he passed."

He looked aghast for a moment, and then he startled her by bursting into laughter. "You climbed a tree?"

She put her hands on her hips, wincing when she scraped her abraded palm anew, and glared up at him. "Truly, I did." As an afterthought, she looked down to ensure she had pulled the hem of her dress from her bodice, and to her great relief, she must have done so automatically after getting out of the tree.

"Anyway, after he left, I looked in the building, and it is where he is hiding his stash of stolen goods. I recognized Mrs. St. Croix's lace and Mr. Cravvy's straight razor among the things."

"Excellent. We must speak with Constable Walters at once."

She frowned. "Do you not want to inspect the items yourself?"

He tilted his head slightly. "Why would I need to do that?"

Lizzy was honestly puzzled. "You are prepared to accept my word on the matter?"

He seemed amused. "Is there some reason I should not be? Is this an elaborate ruse to make me look like a buffoon?"

She could have made a cutting remark about his lack of needing assistance in that department after the impression he'd made at the Assembly ball, but she kept the words to herself. She was still startled by his trust, and in fact so startled she didn't think to protest returning to Meryton and finding Constable Walters until they were near Goliath.

"I am not a horsewoman, and Constable Walters is unlikely to be of any use."

"We must inform the proper authorities, Miss Bennet." With those words, he mounted the horse with perfect grace.

"I shall just stay here and wait for your return."

With an impatient sigh, he bent down and put his arm around her shoulders, lifting her up as she cried out in protest. It was a temporary sound she quickly muffled as she regained control of her senses, finding herself tucked uncomfortably in front of Darcy on his English saddle when she would have preferred a sidesaddle. "This is most unusual, Mr. Darcy."

"Everything about the situation is entirely unusual, Miss Bennet." He spoke briskly and entreated Goliath to start running. They soon arrived in Meryton.

Lizzy was self-conscious about riding through town on a shared horse with Mr. Darcy, but she couldn't allow it to distract her from the task at hand. He stopped outside the constable's building moments later, dismounting first before helping her down. Her bum was throbbing slightly from the unaccustomed exercise, and she was glad it had been less than two miles.

The constable came out of the office, likely hearing the horse arrive, or perhaps he was drawn by the spectacle of seeing Miss Bennet riding one, since it was well known she had no interest in horses. It wasn't that she wasn't interested. They were simply incompatible with her comfort level, being so large and capable of injury, and her being so uneasy and incompetent around them.

Speaking of incompetence, the constable reacted much as she had expected. "I shall retrieve the items and redistribute them to the proper owners then. Thank you for your assistance, Mr. Darcy."

Lizzy scowled, not missing he completely disregarded her contribution to the situation. That hardly surprised her though, since he was a typical man. She cleared her throat. "Do you not think it would be wiser to leave the items where they are and set up an ambush? You could wait until he returns to add to his stash or take something away and catch him in the act."

The constable sneered. "I have better things to do than waste hours sitting in the woods."

"Is that not your job?" asked Lizzy with a tone that was entirely too sweet to be convincingly polite.

Even Walters, thick as he was, recognized the insult in her tone. "I know what my job is, Missy, and it is not indulging spoiled brats."

Lizzy stiffened, but Darcy put a hand on her shoulder, speaking for her, which she also resented. "Constable Walters, would you be agreeable to leaving the items there for at least one more day? I should very much like to observe the area to see if our thief returns."

Walters appeared to consider the matter for a moment. "You will be the one waiting out there to see if he comes back?"

"I shall."

After a moment, the constable shrugged in a careless way. "Do enjoy yourself, Mr. Darcy. The people who have been stolen from have waited this long. I do not suppose it will matter another day, and I confess my rheumatism is acting up something awful today. Yes, I should quite enjoy not having to fetch the items until tomorrow." He shot Darcy a considering look. "Unless you plan to deliver them yourself, sir?"

Darcy's expression turned frigid. "I do not, Constable. Tomorrow should be expedient enough for you to retrieve them."

The man looked disappointed, but he nodded. "Of course, sir." He didn't even acknowledge Lizzy, which was beyond the pale, as he turned and went back into the small office used by the constable.

Lizzy glared after him before turning her glare on Darcy. "I can speak for myself."

"You can, and I have no doubt you were going to suggest a similar solution, but a man like Walters would take it better coming from me. I suspect part of him would be inflexible and insist on arguing the matter just because you are a woman."

If that did not drain her anger, she couldn't think of what might. She was marveling at his perceptiveness and how much trust he'd placed in her to start with by not insisting on examining the stolen goods himself. "We shall return to set up our camp. It needs to be somewhere discreet, but close enough we can approach him if he appears."

He frowned. "I will not allow you to put yourself in danger, Miss Bennet. I shall see to this task alone, or perhaps ask my valet to attend with me."

She glared at him. "I fail to see how you can stop me, Mr. Darcy. If you do not wish to share a lookout, I shall simply find my own. I can still climb a tree, though I do not know about you."

He looked irritated for a moment before his expression cleared. "What of your reputation, Miss Bennet? The two of us spending time alone in the woods without a proper chaperone? That would be scandalous. You could be ruined."

She grimaced. "I believe the excitement of finding the burglar will certainly overshadow any gossip that might arise from the two of us working together to bring the villain to justice. It is a risk I am prepared to take."

He sniffed. "I am not, Miss Bennet. Return to Longbourn." With those words, he turned to Goliath, mounted the horse, and rode away.

Lizzy resisted the urge to stick out her tongue and stomp her foot. She was too mature for such antics, but the man drove her to the point of tantrum in her rage. Shaking her head at his heavy-handed command, as though she would listen to him, she squared her shoulders and started walking. She knew exactly where she was going, and she arrived only a little while after him.

Lizzy made a point of finding herself a perch that was not near him, though she was aware of him watching her. It wasn't the most comfortable spot, but the rotted log she had taken residence on had the benefit of being shielded by a fall of leaves from an overgrown tree that hung down under the burden of its branches and leaves. It was still possible to be seen, but not likely, especially if the thief wasn't expecting someone to be waiting to ensnare them.

Darcy was a stubborn man, but he had come running as soon Lizzy found the villain, so he was reliable. His perch was close enough to allow him to intercept the thief, and she reluctantly admitted she was glad to have him involved in the situation. There was reassurance in having him nearby, though she would never admit that to him. She would feel just as relieved to have any man in the vicinity to back her up when it came time to confront the thief, she assured herself.

Watching for a robber to return was dreadfully boring, and soon, her buttocks were tingling from the position in which she sat. Lizzy had to relieve herself, so she looked around, verifying Darcy had not left his spot, and found a discreet place in the woods.

After finishing, she returned quietly, not wanting to disturb the thief in case he was there, and she was almost back to her perch when a hand clamped around her mouth while another dragged her back against a body. She stiffened in alarm, but at the same time, she could summon no fear. There was something familiar about the body against hers, and by the scent of the man, she immediately knew it was Darcy.

"That is how easy it is to overcome you, Miss Bennet. I implore you to do the wise thing and return home."

As soon as he released her, she took a step away, though she was strangely reluctant to do so. She spun and stared up at him. "I am not going anywhere, Mr. Darcy."

He heaved a sigh of impatience. "Of course not, for though you are intelligent, you make terrible choices."

She shrugged a shoulder. "I do not require your good opinion of me, Mr. Darcy."

He curled his lip. "That is good, because once you have lost my good opinion, you are unable to ever reobtain it."

She shook her head, feigning sadness. "How uncomfortable it must be to be so narrowminded and certain of all your impressions that you never reevaluate them."

He was glaring now. "You have given me no reason to reevaluate my opinion of you, Miss Bennet."

She shrugged. "I am certainly torn up about that, Mr. Darcy, but there are far more important things on which we must focus now. I suggest you return to your hole, and I shall do the same."

With another sigh of impatience, he lifted the branches for her in what she supposed was the gentlemanly equivalent of opening her door. She slipped under, surprised when he followed her. She gave him a look of shock. "What are you doing?"

"Your hiding place is better than mine," he said with a hint of rancor in his tone. "It provides a better view of the area while shielding our presence more effectively."

Lizzy supposed she could abandon her spot, but she decided to take the more mature approach and nod her head. "Very good." She was doing her best not to grin like an idiot at having found the better spot, though he seemed to realize her struggle, because his eyes narrowed, and his lips had closed into a thin line of disapproval.

Lizzy took her spot on the log, sliding over as far as she could to make room for Darcy to sit beside her. It was certainly improper sitting like this with him, and she couldn't recall being this close to any man, other than her father. Of course, there was nothing improper about the situation, other than the inherent shock of her being part of an operation to find the thief and catch him in the act.

She could well imagine her mother's horror at the idea, but she suspected her father, though he would not approve of her risking her safety, would have a little chuckle at the concept at least. He might even envy her the adventure.

Not that there was much adventure involved as they whiled away the rest of the afternoon slowly. Lizzy's stomach grumbled more than once, but when Darcy suggested they stop for food and return later, she refused. "You are free to have a break if you would like, Mr. Darcy, but one of us should remain here at all times."

He shook his head. "Do you anticipate taking down the robber on your own then, Miss Bennet? I wonder why you did not do so earlier if that is your plan?"

She glared at him. "I simply meant one of us should be here to keep watch."

His lips twitched, and she suspected he was deliberately provoking her. Cranky as she was from hunger, she thought he might be risking his life in a different way, but she held back an angry retort.

Most of the afternoon passed in silence, though they occasionally exchanged conversation about various benign topics. She was surprised to discover they had similar tastes in music and reading, as she never would have anticipated sharing any true commonalities with Mr. Darcy.

As the sun started to set, Darcy moved restlessly. "I believe it is time to yield for today, Miss Bennet. I must get you home before dark, and it seems unlikely our thief will be returning tonight. Even if Constable Walters reclaims the items and redistributes them, we might yet catch him returning to the shed."

Lizzy sniffed. "Constable Walters is incompetent and lazy. He is likely to leave the cart of items to be reclaimed out front and post an announcement throughout the village to do so. As soon as Constable Walters reclaims these items, our thief might as well have the announcement in his hand that there is no point in returning, and we shall not catch him."

He frowned. "I concede the point, but I cannot have you out after dark in my company alone. It would be unseemly."

"I understand that, and I do not wish to risk my reputation or yours, and Lord knows the last thing I would want is to be forced into marriage with you, Mr. Darcy, but I suggest we wait a little longer."

He scowled, but after a moment, his shoulders slumped. "Twenty more minutes, and that is all, Miss Bennet. At seven p.m., I am taking you home."

Since he stated it is a fact, she felt no need to agree. He seemed to accept her silence as a promise or consent, but she would decide at seven o'clock if she was ready to go, or if she planned to stay longer. Part of her recognized her obstinacy was simply a reaction to Mr. Darcy and the feelings he engendered in her. The man was maddening, and he made her want to be contrary just for the sake of contrariness.

The minutes ticked past, and she was well aware of Darcy watching them, because he did not put away his pocket watch. He kept it open the entire time, and once seventeen minutes had passed, he looked like he was going to stand up again. "There are still three minutes," she said in a mild tone.

He lifted his hand. "Shush."

Lizzy's mouth parted, and it was her first instinct to argue, because she thought he was shushing her in a very rude fashion because he was intent on leaving, but then she heard footsteps approaching. She immediately closed her mouth and remained quiet as their thief neared the building.

Mr. Darcy jumped beside her when the woods screeched against each other, and she wished she'd thought to warn him. Thankfully, he had the discretion not to make a sound, and she had been expecting it in an unconscious sort of way. They heard it close a moment later, and Lizzy turned slightly, observing the man had entered the building and closed the door behind him.

"I want you to take Goliath and get help. I shall stay here and keep him locked in the building."

Lizzy shook her head frantically. "I cannot ride your horse. I do not know how, Mr. Darcy. I promise you, I am a fast runner, and it will not be much more delay for me to run to Longbourn."

He shook his head. "Go to town. Try to get Walters, or perhaps Colonel Forster. I suspect our thief is one of his men, so it makes sense to involve him."

Lizzy understood his reasoning, but she doubted Walters would be any help. She felt a moment of anxiety as she stared at him before starting to leave the cover of the trees. Darcy was right behind her, and he was slipping toward the building.

She wanted to tell him to be careful, inexplicably worried about his safety on a level she shouldn't be, but she quelled the urge, both because it was so foreign, and because she didn't want to alert their robber they had found him and were planning to lock him in. With one last glance at Darcy, she turned and ran, abandoning any hope of being ladylike in favor of speed, which was far more important at the moment.

Chapter Nine

Darcy leaned closer, inadvertently pressing his weight too much against the wood and causing it to screech as he tried to brace the door. It had been his intent to engage the latch, but now, he'd alerted the thief inside that he was there. He braced his weight against it, expecting the man to throw himself against the door. Nothing happened for a moment, and then there was a cracking sound followed by breaking wood.

Darcy had braced himself, so it was anticlimactic when there was no collision with the door itself. Rather, the man had thrown his weight against one rickety side of the shed, and he burst through in a spray of splinters and old rotted boards. Darcy was unsurprised to see Wickham standing in front of him, and he rushed after the other man.

He tackled him to bring him to the ground, and Wickham turned, trying to hit him. They scuffled for a bit on the ground, and Darcy almost had the advantage when Wickham brought up his knee in a savage motion, driving it forcefully into Darcy's groin. Pain like he had never experienced flared through him, and he couldn't maintain his grasp on the other man.

Instead, he rolled to the side, allowing Wickham to gain his feet. He expected Wickham to kick him while he was down, or further try to incapacitate him, so he was doing his best to breathe through the agony and sit up, but Wickham must have deemed it more important to escape than to get revenge, because he ran.

Darcy was still in agony, but he had managed to get to his knees when Lizzy returned moments later in the company of Colonel Forster, with that bumbling Walters riding behind, complaining the whole way about this being a waste of his time when he was just about to eat dinner.

Lizzy had ridden with the colonel, and he handed her down before she ran to Darcy. He couldn't explain the warmth he felt inside when she knelt beside him, touching his shoulder. "What happened, Mr. Darcy?"

"Wickham is no gentleman when it comes to fighting."

Colonel Forster ran right behind her, and he saw the man wince, clearly intuiting the meaning of his words. Dear Lizzy clearly did not, and she frowned. "I do not understand."

"That is all right, Miss Bennet. I shall have a soldier take you home while Mr. Darcy and I sort this out."

"I am not going anywhere yet, Colonel Forster. I am the one who discovered the thief's stash, and I deserve to see what happens."

The colonel looked prepared to argue with her, but then he shrugged. "Did you identify the thief, Mr. Darcy?"

He watched her face, realizing she might not have understood what he was saying before when he called Wickham by name. "It was George Wickham, sir. I exchanged enough blows with him to be certain of that. You will find further proof of the fact because his nose is bleeding copiously." He spoke to the colonel, but his gaze remained on Lizzy. He expected her to reject his claim, though she had seemed to believe his warning about Wickham once he'd explained the man's true nature.

Instead, she was frowning down at him with concern. "You are bleeding from the lip, Mr. Darcy." She reached boldly into his pocket, taking the handkerchief there, and turned her tender ministrations on him. He was surprised by how gently she dabbed his lip, and it caused an uncomfortable and unfamiliar sensation to squeeze his chest.

He found it almost difficult to breathe for a moment, but he finally managed to draw in a lungful of air and exhale raggedly. That caused his body to hurt again, particularly in his swollen anatomy, and he wanted for nothing but a tub full of ice. He doubted they could acquire enough at short notice to fill an entire tub, but perhaps at least a bagful.

The colonel still seemed sympathetic as he gestured for one of his men. Darcy listened while he authorized the man to send out troops to find Wickham and arrest him on sight.

Walters came forward then. "Do you still need me? I have dinner to get to."

The colonel seemed as impatient as Fitzwilliam felt, and Lizzy had clearly reached the end of her perseverance with him as well. "You still have these belongings to return to people," she said in a tight voice.

Walters seemed unconcerned. "That can wait 'til morning, Miss Bennet. Perhaps the colonel can post a guard here if he's worried about theft."

With a sigh of disgust, the colonel said, "Return to your post, man. I shall handle this."

With a sigh of relief, Walters turned back to retrieve his horse. He mounted the swaybacked mare who had clearly seen better days and started cantering back to Meryton.

After discussing the situation with the colonel, sharing what they had both learned in the process, Darcy was finally able to gain his feet. He was uncertain about riding Goliath, but it was still the fastest way back to Longbourn and Netherfield, so he gingerly mounted the horse after lifting Elizabeth onto the saddle.

She was unhappy with the situation, but he didn't feel like he could walk several miles in his current state, and of course, he couldn't allow her to go home unassisted. The colonel was busy with the situation here, so it fell to him to do the right thing. He was surprised that she barely argued the issue, and she seemed slightly more at ease on Goliath's back as they cantered slowly toward Longbourn. Darcy couldn't handle a fast jolt at the moment.

"I am sorry he bested you, Mr. Darcy."

He sighed. "As am I." Particularly in the method Wickham had used.

"I mean that in a genuine way. It was not to highlight your inability to stop him."

"I do think you for clarifying. I am never quite sure exactly what you mean, Miss Bennet, though I can always infer it is nothing complementary."

She straightened again. "You did come when I asked you to, and you eventually saw reason and submitted to my plan. I must thank you for those things, for we would not know it is Mr. Wickham without you."

"Your praise is most refreshing. Parsimonious perhaps, but I appreciate the gesture."

She harrumphed at him, and he struggled not to smile. Despite the pain radiating from his lower body, he felt unexpectedly light. It was a motion he would identify as happiness if it weren't caused by Miss Bennet, who bore him nothing but ill will. That he could enjoy her company, especially under these circumstances, was shocking.

When they returned to Longbourn, they found Mr. Bennet pacing frantically in front of the house. He came rushing forward, practically jerking Lizzy off the horse and hugging her in a tight embrace for a moment before stepping back. "Are you uninjured, child?"

"I am, Papa. Mr. Darcy did not fare so well."

He braced himself for the shame of Elizabeth revealing the full extent of his injuries, wondering if she even comprehended them herself. Despite the situation, he couldn't help a hint of amusement at the idea of her explaining testicular injury to her father.

His amusement fled when he met Mr. Bennet's gaze. The other man was enraged, and though Darcy wouldn't have expected the man to have it in him, clearly, there was another side of Thomas Bennet that was more than the aloof, slightly sarcastic man. Darcy straightened his shoulders. "Nothing untoward happened, Mr. Bennet. We were caught up in the excitement of catching a thief."

Mr. Bennet's eyes widened. "Indeed? Is that true, Lizzy?"

"Oh, it is, Papa. Come inside, and I shall tell you." She paused, looking at Fitzwilliam. "Would you like to join us, Mr. Darcy?"

The idea of ice and rest was far too tempting to lure him away from it, especially to explain the situation to Mr. Bennet. "I have every faith in your ability to truthfully convey what happened and to portray me in the most negative light possible, Miss Bennet. I shall bid you good evening."

She surprised him with her lips trembling for a moment before she smiled. He quickly turned Goliath toward Netherfield, but he was unaccountably pleased that he had managed to get through her shell enough to make her smile with his comment. His aim had been to make her laugh, but that was close enough.

He touched the brim of his hat and bent his head in her direction and Mr. Bennet's before turning and riding home to Netherfield.

Slowly.

Ever so slowly.

Chapter Ten

Lizzy repeated the story for Jane a couple of hours later, after Papa had given her leave to go to bed. He'd wanted to hear more than once how she'd put it all together, and he'd seemed pleased by Mr. Darcy's contribution, though he clearly recognized Lizzy had done the lion's share of the work. "You are my clever girl," he'd said after pressing a kiss to her forehead before letting her leave his study. "Do not put yourself in unnecessary danger next time though."

"I swear I did not at all, Papa. Mr. Darcy bore the brunt of the danger."

Her father had winced unaccountably, though she couldn't understand why. "Indeed, he did."

Lizzy wanted to ask for clarification, but she sensed it would be useless. When she'd tried earlier upon relaying what Mr. Darcy's words had been about his injury, her father had winced in a similar fashion, but he had refused to elucidate the subject for her. He'd simply placated her with the information that sometimes, there were things a lady would never understand and didn't need to know.

Now, she wound down the tale, and Jane looked more frightened than her father had. Mr. Bennet had been more awed by the experience, whereas Jane was clearly letting anxiety get the best of her. "Oh, Lizzy, you could have been dreadfully injured."

"Mr. Darcy was there to help me."

Jane frowned. "You were alone with Mr. Darcy in the woods all that time?"

She flushed slightly. "Yes, but you do not need to reveal that part to Papa. I led him to believe it was more of an unexpected situation. Mr. Darcy and I had run into each other as I was leaving Meryton and he was heading that way, but he offered to walk me home. We came across a burglar entering the building, recognized the goods, and Mr. Darcy volunteered to stay behind to ensure he didn't escape." She lowered her voice. "You understand why I do not want the full story to get out. I do not wish to have people assume there was something sordid about it, nor do I want to be forced to marry Fitzwilliam Darcy."

Jane tilted her head, giving Lizzy a look that was far too penetrative. "Despite your protests, I suspect you like Mr. Darcy."

Lizzy's eyes widened. "I never said I did not like him." She flushed, recalling just how obvious her dislike had been after the assembly ball, and the number of times she had brought him up in an unfavorable light that evening and since. "I suppose I do not like him, but he is not as bad as I thought."

"I am glad you are giving him a second chance."

Lizzy frowned. "There was hardly anything to it, Jane. We simply united for a common goal. It is not as though we are going to become dear friends and spend hours together endeavoring to catch criminals. Besides, he would be an unsuitable partner. He allowed Mr. Wickham to escape."

Jane frowned. "It seems to be through no fault of his own. Papa was sympathetic for whatever reason."

Lizzy shrugged. "I agree, but if a man has an area that sensitive, he can hardly be relied upon for protection. Someone facing off with him would simply need to exploit the spot."

Jane frowned. "What do you think the spot is?"

Lizzy flushed and looked down. "I do not know specifically, but I suspect it is something in the general region of...there." She waved her hand over her pelvis, and Jane's eyes widened. "Mr. Darcy was cradling that particular area when I found him with Colonel Forster."

"I see. I wonder how a man is different from a woman? I suppose it would be a sensitive area, but do you think a woman can be incapacitated in a similar fashion?"

Lizzy shrugged. "I have no idea, and I am not eager to find out. Truly, I do not see such an occurrence happening again. This is most certainly a one-off, and Mr. Darcy would be the last person I would choose to partner with for such future endeavors even if I were to willfully seek them out, I assure you."

"If you say so." Jane seemed unconvinced, but apparently, she decided not to tease Lizzy. She must have recognized her sister's exhaustion.

There was no denying it, and Lizzy laid down in her bed a short time later, fully expecting to fall asleep right away. Instead, the evening's events played through her mind, and she was startled to find she was more concerned about Mr. Darcy than she'd expected, especially knowing the outcome. He was clearly going to recover just fine, so she did her best to banish him from her thoughts.

After some struggle, she managed to fall asleep, and she dreamed of walking with Mr. Darcy in the same meadow where they had stopped the burglar. This time, the sun was shining down upon them, her hand was tucked in his, and they were pressed far too closely together to be proper.

The dream caused her to wake with a smile, though she firmly refused to admit dreaming of him had left her in such a fine mood as she got up to prepare for the day. Whatever had occurred with Mr. Darcy was certainly never going to happen again.

This series needs to be read in order, just like Jane Austen's masterpiece.
The series in order:
Rapacity & Rancor[1]

<u>Abduction & Acrimony</u>[2]
<u>Extortion & Enmity</u>[3]
<u>Murder & Misjudgment</u>[4]
<u>Perfidy & Promises</u>[5]

PLEASE SIGN UP FOR Abbey's newsletter[6] to receive information about new releases. If you have any difficulties, email Abbey to request a manual add.

---

1. https://books2read.com/u/4ApM1d

2. https://books2read.com/u/mBwB1k

3. https://books2read.com/u/bxQGPe

4. https://books2read.com/u/bzZyAn

5. https://books2read.com/u/mddaAE

6. https://www.subscribepage.com/JAFF

About The Author

Abbey is a diehard Jane Austen fan and has loved Fitzwilliam since the first time she "met" him at age thirteen upon borrowing the book from the school library. He is the ideal man, though Abbey's husband is a close second. Abbey enjoys writing various steamy and sweet Jane Austen variations, but "Pride & Prejudice" (and Mr. Darcy) will always be her favorite.

Did you love *Rapacity & Rancor: A Pride & Prejudice Variation*? Then you should read *Abduction & Acrimony : A Pride & Prejudice Variation Mystery Romance*[1] by Abbey North!

[2]

Everyone in Meryton is excited about the upcoming Netherfield ball, but Lizzy is preoccupied, for the thief, though his identity is known, is still at-large. When Mr. Darcy's sister arrives, she and Lizzy become fast friends, but Lizzy's acrimony with Darcy threatens everything, especially when she overhears him condemning Jane as a grasping social climber without true regard for Bingley. They are at odds, but when an abduction occurs the very night of the ball, it brings the two of them together to find the kidnapper and rescue his victim. Will they find a tenuous accord, or will their continued animosity keep them separated?

---

1. https://books2read.com/u/mBwB1k

2. https://books2read.com/u/mBwB1k

Also by Abbey North

A Month To Love
Reproach (Part One)
Resentment (Part Two)
Rapport (Part Three)
A Month To Love Compilation

Crime & Courtship
Rapacity & Rancor: A Pride & Prejudice Variation
Abduction & Acrimony : A Pride & Prejudice Variation Mystery Romance
Extortion & Enmity: A Pride & Prejudice Variation Mystery Romance
Murder & Misjudgment: A Pride & Prejudice Variation Mystery Romance
Perfidy & Promises: A Pride & Prejudice Variation Mystery Romance
Crime & Courtship: A Sweet Pride & Prejudice Mystery Romance Compilation

Darcy's Courtesan
Adversity (Darcy's Courtesan, Part One)

Avidity (Darcy's Courtesan, Part Two)
Amity (Darcy's Courtesan, Part Three)
Darcy's Courtesan: A Sensual "Pride & Prejudice" Variation

Marriage & Mysteries
Honeymoon & Hemlock

Mr. Darcy's Secret Stories
Mistaken Masquerade: A Pride & Prejudice Variation
Mischief & Matchmaking: A "Pride & Prejudice" Variation

Standalone
Christmas At Pemberley: A Pride & Prejudice Variation
A Scandalous Proposition: A Pride & Prejudice Variation
Shadow of Darcy: A Sensual Pride & Prejudice Paranormal Variation
Darcy's Obsession
Blackmailing Lizzy: A "Pride & Prejudice" Variation
Darcy's Wicked Game
Danger With Darcy: A Sensual "Pride & Prejudice" Variation
Passion & Prostrations: A Sensual "Pride & Prejudice" Variation
Darcy's Debt: A Sensual Pride & Prejudice Variation
Obstinacy & Obligation: A Sweet Pride & Prejudice Variation
Darcy's Alibi: A Sweet "Pride & Prejudice" Variation
Marooned With Darcy: A Sensual "Pride & Prejudice" Variation
Compromising Mr. Darcy: A Steamy "Pride & Prejudice" Variation
Marrying Mr. Darcy: A Sensual "Pride & Prejudice" Variation
Darcys' First Christmastide